THE FERN HEDGE

JEAN HARRISON

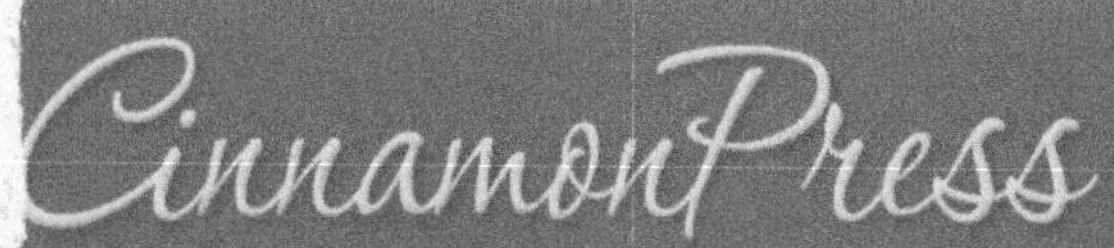

Published by Cinnamon Press
Meirion House,
Tanygrisiau,
Blaenau Ffestiniog
Gwynedd LL41 3SU
www.cinnamonpress.com

The right of Jean Harrison to be identified as author of this work has be
asserted by her in accordance with the Copyright, Designs and Patent
1988. © 2017 Jean Harrison. ISBN 978-1-910836-71-2
British Library Cataloguing in Publication Data. A CIP record for
book can be obtained from the British Library.

Designed and typeset in Garamond by Cinnamon Press. Cover desig
Adam Craig © Adam Craig.; Labyrinth element based on an orig
drawing by Tomas Bednarik © Tomas Bednarik, Dreamstime.com

Cinnamon Press is represented by Inpress and by the Welsh Books Cou
in Wales. Printed in Poland.

The publisher gratefully acknowledges the support of the Welsh Boo
Council.

Acknowledgements

There are so many people who have helped in the production of this book. First of all Barbara who listened to endless variations on the first draft; then Gillian Walton and John Killick who read and commented on a much later second version; Jean Stevens who gave critical attention to scattered chapters; and, of course to Jan Fortune and Adam Craig who supplied editing skills and a lot of much appreciated encouragement. Also to the staff of The Armouries, Leeds who guided me so kindly to information about rifle shooting. As well as them I'd like to thank Maddy Cokell and other members of the Continued Care team who've taken responsibilities off me, allowing me time to get down to the completion of this book. Thanks to all of you.

I should also like to acknowledge the help I've received from the following books:
The People's War, Angus Calder 1969 Pantheon Books
Women in Green, Charles Graves 1948 Heineman
Green Sleeves, Katherine Bentley Beauman 1977 Seeley, Service and co
Dementia Reconsidered, Tom Kitwood 1977 Open University Press
A Beginner's Guide to Fly-tying, Chris Mann and Terry Griffiths 1999 Merlin Unwin Books
And most of all to *Alzheimer's from the inside out* Richard Taylor, Health Professions Press 2007, a moving and revealing account of his experience descending into the disease.

THE FERN HEDGE

1

6.30 a.m.

The green eye stares, calm and cold. The pupil contracts then rapidly expands sending amber flecks rippling across the iris. What is this—this—this—stare? What's it doing? One's forced to return it. There must be a second eye—there are always two—aren't there? Always two. Somewhere hidden—the other side of the hedge. One like this is enough.

Something wrong with the hedge—a hedge of—of? High. Twenty foot? Always be accurate. Fern twenty foot high? A big fern—yes—Dryopteris something—Ae—Aemula—Dryopteris Aemula—the name now wonderfully, mercifully solidifying on air—can always be relied on.

The eye has gone, someone has snatched it away—but something is still there, growling up and down behind the ferns, scraping its claws on the ground, the fronds swaying, flicking their tips out, clutching. Everything shaking. Earthquake? Whatever it is, it's tossing trees into the air, the whole of them, roots and all—one can see the roots, black and waving against the sky—thudding them back down like pestles, while the ferns thrust their fronds sideways, interweave them, link their tiniest fingers to hold that confusion the other side of them, police straining against a mob.

This must be a dream—this time at least—though there are times, times nowadays—but now she must be dreaming—that she, Alice Lomas, is standing there, watching, but at the same time knows she's in danger, with only that lacy green line as protection. There's no way of escape either for her, or for the person she's standing alongside, who's also her. How is that possible? The ferns will never hold.

All at once the earthquake smoothes out and the air with it. Even the growls stop. This is paradise, this quiet. The ferns untwine and gently begin curling and uncurling their fingers.

She lies with her eyes closed, shaking a little, trying to keep this last picture before her eyes, but it fades and leaves only the feeling of having been set free. In a stillness she finds surprising, she hears a thrush, clear and confident, repeating itself on the cool morning air.

Where? Where exactly is that bird? One does like precision—that is the delight of geometry—but the call, though it pierces the curtains, lacks precise geographical location. The song comes simply from outside, from mid-air, from nothingness, but she knows where the singer must be, perched on the weather-vane above the stable. That is where they always sit—and she's seen generations of them in the forty-eight years since she came to Holmbush.

The thread breaks suddenly, not drifting apart the way threads too often do but snapped by noise—brakes, an engine throbbing—ghastly shriek of a motor-cycle—

Charlie—something—loud-mouthed young man—hopeless in the garden—

What's the road doing so close outside the window? What's happened to the drive? The whine saws through walls which seem to be trembling. They need soothing.

She reaches out her left hand, touches nothing, nothing at all, strains her fingers out into emptiness. It's all air. She opens her eyes, turns them in every direction, sees something misty but solid on the right side of the bed. Not where a wall should be. She fishes for her glasses, is aware of pressure from her bladder.

Something's happening today. What day is that? Days have less substance than cobwebs. Sunday? What is it that's happening? It is imperative to grasp what and where. Holmbush. Always Holmbush. This isn't. Isn't what? Isn't right, not right for Holmbush So? Set the mind to the problem. Solutions always to be found. Slowly nowadays. They keep drifting.

Of course—this is—Fay—Fair—Fairview House—names more available this morning—which looks out on those raucous-pink cherries and red buses of—of—of—that—that Avenue—churches, something to do with churches. She pushes herself onto her elbow. Churches? Of course one has no objection to churches, not as names. One is invariably content where one has chosen to be, for it all originates in the will. The will is the great secret, that and reason. She rests for a moment contemplating the window-bars, admiring the way those strong rectangles impose order on a random spread of leaves, branches and sky. For the first time, after a lifetime of giving in, one has known the satisfaction of ordering one's own fate. That's it, all clear now, one has let Kate have Holmbush. January 4th 1978 one handed over Holmbush to Kate.

Kate understands how to polish furniture.

She edges her hip sideways, stops, moves it again, grasps the bar beside the bed and pulls herself up. She takes off her glasses, peers into the lenses, puffs on them, wipes them with her hankie, peers into them again, suspects they're still smeared, puts them on.

The room acquires shape. From the bed in its recess she can see diagonally down and across the main bar of the L to the side of her arm-chair and the ends of bookshelves. Directly facing her, the sun pours three vertical bars of light between and beside the curtains, a silky warmth which reaches into the gloom where she lies, while she inspects her possessions as she does every morning.

She checks them over, one table, one bureau, two chairs, four bookshelves. All there and solid. Count them over again. *Did you check your answer Natasha? Look at this, £300.00 for a season ticket?* Display of lowered lashes, *No, Miss Hearn.*

Miss Hearn?

She's gone. Where? But there was a time—Was she Alice? Alice Hearn? Work at it—clarity, must find it—now—now if she was Alice—no Alice Lomas then? Is Alice Lomas real? One seems to think so. Later then. One must have become Mrs Lomas later. How?

After George stood beside Peggy and Peggy's daughter was with them—Natasha, too ornamental ever to check an answer—just like her mother. George stands beside Peggy, a trim dark cloud on the lawn. Stop skulking, George, were you the answer? *One should always check one's answers.* Two of them and Natasha beside them on the lawn. Mother:daughter, brother:sister, uncle:niece. One male:two females. One can't balance the equation. George beside Peggy. Peggy beside George. He's not here today.

This morning's good. There is a pleasing precision. They furniture may conceivably be crammed a little too close for comfort. That keeps everything firm. The table exactly fits the space between the windows. The end of the bed makes a satisfying straight line across the side of the bureau. A straight line is the shortest distance—but that bureau—an excellent piece. In his study between his bookshelves. Kate understands polishing but she can't have Father's bureau. It was in his study but she insists on teaching Domestic Science in one of those schools—a school yes—she insists on Domestic Science in a school that's a dumping ground for the brainless. She can be roped in to polish. Polishing is not of the essence.

The frown lines between her eyes break. She can see everything so clearly this morning. Polishing is not of the essence. Simplicity is—a bed, two armchairs, a table, dining chairs, books and father's bureau. All framed by the clarity of white walls.

The bladder. That involves slippers. Where? Kate hopeless from the first. Small child repeating she couldn't, she couldn't. Crying over something quite simple; mewed and bleated for weeks over this *problem. Are you sure you'll like the home, Mummy? Do you think you'll be happy there?* Happiness. Happiness is not of the essence. She pushes back the bedclothes, lowers her legs.

There's no need for you to go, Mummy. Really, genuinely, we'd love to have you. Think what would a wrench it would be to leave Holmbush after all these years. Holbush not of the essence. Where are those slippers? *We could remodel the stables. You'd have your own rooms and all your things round you. John and Jo and I can easily fit into the house.* £300 for a season ticket? Did you check your answer? Should be 4,1,1978.

George never an answer. One was drawn to him once. No truth, however painful, should be evaded. The bladder.

Ah, that's the slippers. Bare feet gleam up at her, long, narrow, white. *Aristocratic, too good for a schoolmarm. Don't be so silly, George. George, take me away from that school.* Did you check your answer? Take one away—leaves what? Holes in stockings and coloured hair-ribbons? The school defended civilisation against them. One had hoped to teach girls to be rational.

She starts to cram these distinguished feet into slippers whose backs flatten under her heels, entangle the hem of her nightdress. She tries to scoop it out with a fore-finger. A wrench, Kate said, as if that meant something. Happiness is not of the essence. When—since arriving here —six months ago, January 4th 1978—figures always reliable. Some things are so confusing—one is afraid sometimes—but figures, see how clearly they come?—the day before Kate's forty-fourth birthday and how she mewed and bleated—*we'd love to have you with us—Kate, your answer's a hole in a stocking*—when has one ever given a single thought to Holmbush?

She launches herself onto her legs. Some women in this house make a big thing of telling everyone their age showing off how spry they are. Showing off. Vulgar. That man—George, that's it, George, same as the king—fancied himself at tennis. King of the tennis court. *Up to the net, Alice. Leave the back line to me.* One played tennis. Gardened too. Only once on a horse. Children watching. Don't make a fool of oneself. That girl spends far too much time with that pony.

Shows signs of a brain.

It has to be admitted—physically speaking, one's own performance nowadays, even across this room, is disappointing.

By this time she's reached the window and drawn back the curtains. Light takes over. She can see the mahogany wardrobe, the pie-crust table, the oriental carpet, rows of books. One doesn't look at that object in the corner. Miss McDonald insisted, as if one was not capable of dealing with one's needs. She turns for the door.

The other side of it brown carpet stretches trackless in both directions. One has always been decisive, so right, one foot in front of the other. Cream walls, couple of windows one side, row of brown doors the other. That oval porcelain plaque not on this one. Nor the next. Why not?

A blank wall springs up in front of her. She gazes at it slowly. Of course one knows where one's going. All the same, how did it get here? Jumping up like that in front of one. One turned right—or left—anyway one turned and this wall appeared. So where? Where?

Of course there's no problem. No real problem. She turns, retraces her steps. One's concentration—not quite—

All one needs, concentration. The lavatory can't possibly have taken to hiding itself. How could a lavatory do that? One must be able to find it. Labelled on the door, WC in black letters. Must find it—find it, before Miss McDonald or any of her minions appears. Get upset if they catch one going to the lavatory, as if there's some difficulty, as if it weren't a basic human need. She wants to bring that thing so that it's always standing in the room. One told her emphatically no.

Here at last, two black eyes in a white face. Porcelain. A hard-faced saint.

A quarter of an hour later she stops at the head of the stairs, taking time—and why not? Nothing wrong with one's breathing, it's just that air's short round here. So much short round here. Not time though, plenty of that. Not infinite of course, thought seems to run slowly here. Not the days. They go fast. Relatively.

Something to do with relativity. She comes to a standstill with sunshine filtered by a heavy lace curtain softly outlining her hair and shoulders, gazes down over the banisters to a plant on the landing at the turn of the stairs. There's something about it.

Soon she's close enough to see the pattern of fronds that hide the top of the pot. Lean forward, one can get glimpses of the perfect circle there underneath the interruptions. Stand back, see sides curving like a dumpy capital S. It stands on a rectangular cloth laid on an octagonal table. Lovely, precise technical terms. See how easily they flow.

Then colours get in the way, reflected by sudden sunlight though the leaded lights of the upper panes, leaf-shapes pulled out and distorted by the angle of the sun, blobs without defined edges, floating between her and the fern.

She probes through them to the pot. How did it get here? Miss McDonald of all people? Did one bring it oneself? Surely not Kate. Couldn't be Kate. Not her. So who? Very puzzling but really it's the fern. Wrinkles cut down round her eyes, across her cheeks, at the corners of her eyes, lips draw together, she gazes down; unbrushed hair is dappled with red and blue. There was an article. That demonstrated something—to do with curves; the way little leaves zig-zag; the way their size increases regularly to the mid-point. An article about—this kind of thing. Look, the size decreases to the fine nib of a tip. She strokes a series of acutely angled scalene triangles. It means—what does it mean? Something. One was thinking something—the same came into it, but different. There was an article.

One stood beside a border of ordinary, unsightly ferns, growing in a dusty corner of a common-place garden. Light seemed to shine round. Because of what had been written. An article that had been written, demonstrating. Something. Today there's a feeling of slip and slide but stand here, keep a hold, underneath, looking at this fern all's well. There's reason to it. An article about fractals.

Mathematics. That's it. One's life.

A local accent travels harshly up the stairwell. 'What you doing down here, Muriel? Not breakfast time, you know. Get back to your room.'

Alice takes a sharp breath. That woman a good sight too familiar. Only a kitchen assistant. Miss McDonald knows? Surely not. She may be somewhat tiresome but she'd never use one's Christian name. That poor creature—Miss—Miss—Ingram lets herself in for it. Wandering again, always wandering, talking rubbish. One of the trials of this place. One must not dwell on it. Not on that kind of thing. She gathers her dressing gown round her, starts to plant one foot in front of the other, pulling on the banister. Rational. One is always rational.

'I told you to stay in your room.' Someone said that once. Not downstairs. Came from above. One was looking up, hearing.

7.15 a.m.

Before she opens her eyes, Joanne's thinking about Kate Bush, aching to hear a voice you can't say anything about—except it's not like anything else you've ever heard, just absolutely, wonderfully different.

She slips out from the sheets, heads straight to the disk she wants, takes it from the sleeve, and, holding it between the first fingers of both hands, drops it gently over the upright of the record-player, touches the arm and hesitates. Mum went ballistic last time. She rootles round in the cupboard, fishes out a blanket, grabs a packet of Bluetack from her desk, pulls off a chunk one-handed, stretches on tip-toe, attaches a row of adhesive patches onto the herringbone edging, pushes it with all her weight onto the lintel so it hangs, a little lop-sided, covering the whole door. She stands, looking it over, frowning, tugs one edge over the crack between the door and its frame, tries to pat it into place, thinks of her mother in her room on the floor below. Kate Bush isn't Rock. Not Heavy Metal either if you have to underline the obvious. And it's obvious any sound's going to go up not down. Dad won't wake.

If he did hear something would it matter? That voice at a distance—so totally magic. You have to be with it, in a place you've ever been before; you're so utterly drawn in, just absolutely know that's what life is.

She guides the arm down onto the disk, waits.

The first chords fill the room, she draws into herself, waiting and tingling, and then the voice comes, from high up, far away, a hawk circling in a windy place, Wuthering Heights, wherever that is and Cathy's pleading, *It's me, come home, come home,* but she's dead now and when she was alive Heathcliff could never be right for her—home isn't always where you most need to be and this voice calls strangely, *Let me in, let me in,* as if there's some other place to get into, somewhere that could be different.

The song ends, she starts it again, swaying, loosening her arms, stretching them overhead to all corners of the room, letting them fall back and circle up, shakes out her hair, pictures a slim body, arms, legs, flying dark curls. She closes her eyes, lets herself go.

This time when the music finishes she flings her arms onto the window-sill gazing out into the sun-lit garden: terrace walls that soft red brick Mum has to call 'rosy'—making it sound fancy—cypress on the top terrace, lawn sloping down to the beech tree rising out of the bottom hedge, steps of herringbone brick going down between lavender and geraniums. Holmbush is lovely—of course—but—

Wuthering Heights. That's a strange book, about people who aren't everyday and sensible—but alive. They live every single moment and that way of really living makes things dangerous—which could be better than being stifled with lavender.

Back Lane was a normal, ordinary place. Where I was born —well almost. Actually born in hospital but—all the rest of my life there with my own room looking down over the plum tree—till now, though if you think of it, Holmbush's bigger but in lots of ways not that different. There are other places—different, grim—not just moors but inner cities, tower blocks. Beyond this house and garden, this village with its shop that sells *Almost Everything* (but can't come up with pop-studs) there are people who struggle to live at all. They stare at you from telly. You hear about them in Social Studies. *Cathy, Come Home*—there's something wrong with that title—it's changed the meaning—you need to find out, to understand. When? How? Mum and Dad seem to imagine Holmbush and Gilbridge are the centre of the world—stifled in lavender?

Does that happen to everyone if they stay here too long?

Suddenly she flicks her hair back out of her eyes. Nutmeg'll be waiting with his head over the gate.

She considers re-starting the music while she dresses, instead tears off her pyjamas, throws them on the bed, pulls on bra, panties, jeans, tee-shirt, picks up her trainers, pulls the blanket off the door, opens it, looks up and down the landing, runs downstairs swinging the shoes by the laces, snatches a couple of apples from the bowl on the sideboard, slows to consider Mum's shining masterpiece, standing there silent on its board of silver card.

Can just see the icing through one of those old-fashioned net cloths Mum trots out from somewhere. As birthday cakes go, it has its points—some people'd call it brilliant—but—a complete, utter waste of time—crinkly violet columns round the sides, ribbed violet rim round the top, eight violets, each with four petals. Spooky. Gran has a thing about roses.

Cake's been sitting there on the dresser to dry for days, Mum getting agitated if I get within two feet of it, as if I can't be trusted not to spoil the icing or push it off the worktop. I'm not a kid—though I have looked, not thinking, just looking. Really, really wouldn't touch it. Gran absolutely destined to hate it.

She shrugs, spins on her toe out of the back-door into the garden. A bird is singing. She stops to track where it is. The stable roof, of course. She throws her head back, the air cooling her cheeks and arms, the sun already warm on her shoulders.

People say blackbirds have local accents. Check in Gilbridge this afternoon. While Gran's going on and Mum's saying, 'Yes Mummy, no Mummy,' as if she was a little kid—listen to find out if blackbirds there say the same thing as here.

There's a run to the call, a kind of coolness like a small river; it's less warm and bubbly than Nutmeg's whicker. He'll call you—with the same sound he makes to another pony? Or a little different? The same pattern of sound but different tones? He knows you're his friend. But his language? How could you work it out?

The white-washed stable looks dark after the brightness outside. She feels the rounded shape of brick under her feet, listens again for the blackbird, breathes in the mixed scent of hay and meal. How could Mum and Dad possibly have wanted to convert this into a granny flat when it was completely, totally obvious Gran wouldn't have a thing to do with the idea? Mum wouldn't let the idea drop—on and on as if something was biting her, trying to get Dad to go along with her, and him getting caught up, talking about *partition walls, a window under the eaves, plumbing no real problem,* neither of them thinking about Nutmeg. How could they? How could they leave him outside all winter?

Icicles grew from Gran's eyes. *I've told you what I've decided.* She was right. That time at least.

She reaches down the halter and sets off down the track behind the stable, a green and white world where her trainers make no noise, full of damp scents—may, cow-parsley, wild garlic. In places she can see through the hedge to a sparkle of buttercups and long grass. The same sparkle touches the leaves at the top of the hedge. When she comes to the wood it falls between the tree-trunks and lights up some of the bluebells, though most of them are drifting in shade under the young leaves. Then she comes back into full sun in a place outside the garden, a clearing full of wild creatures, like that squirrel, sitting up on its tail under the oak-tree. Don't move. If I do it'll vanish, put the trunk between me and it. Poke its nose round? Never catch it at it. Just for now it's watching, a few yards away, bright-eyed, nose twitching a little, naughty.

It can go any time it likes. It's free—but for the moment feels safe to stay a close to a human, smelling and observing me out here outside the garden—not penned in the house, not at school, not in the bus going to school but free, walking on damp grass in the real world outside the official places where they put you on tramlines to shunt you through to university—they say I won't become a vet without—and lots of what I do at school's interesting enough in its way, bits I really like—indoors and sitting. *Est-ce-que vous attendez, Joanne?* Crow out there preening itself on top of the telegraph post. *Que fait*—whoever it is on this page of the book? Black feathers shine green in the sun. *Are you listening, Joanne?* Here I'm free to stand and watch a squirrel watching me, free to be alone, free to try to understand things—like those lords-and-ladies there under the hedge with their green hoods and purple spikes inside that are shining not slimy, all the same somehow disgusting, evil. *Disgusted, Tunbridge Wells. What, what.* Silly.

Evil—Emma's kid sister—the one with long red curls and freckles—on the school bus turning round from the seat in front, her eyes gleaming, *totally evil.* You'd think the word was a sweet, way she drew it out—only a kid but I knew what she was feeling—evil being different, weird, something perhaps someone might seek out, turning normal things upside down, finding different eyes.

That strange voice, *Let me in, let me in, let me in.*

Let you in? They won't let a girl train for anything bigger than cats and dogs. Load of old codswallop. Barbed wire trailed through thick grass. Some idiot must have thrown it down and left it. So Nutmeg tore his hock. He was so good, stood there quietly and let me clean it as if he understood. The vet said I'd got it right, in the yard behind his surgery, came out and stood there rubbing his chin, *That'll do. Well done, girl.* And what about rats? Or ferrets?

What Granddad said about them. *Watch out for those teeth.* It's not all down to size.

She stands gazing. Narrow lanes twist up onto moors that touch the sky. Grey stone farmhouses nestle at the foot of bare hills. James Herriot's country. I'll be driving all on my own to help a sheep with a torn ear or a cow in labour.

The squirrel suddenly darts off. Thought I wasn't looking. Wild thing with a life of its own. OK to move now. Indoors all afternoon. A cloud over today. Gilbridge and Gran.

She steps out hurrying along a path that's grown rougher. She can feel the stones through her trainers. 31, Parson's Avenue. Why's that sound so different from 16, Back Street? Both addresses, but totally, totally different. I used to love Back Street.

Gran must've gone barmy choosing that place—dull sort of brown coloured house with a porch up steps that are supposed to look posh but don't. Got to be rational, she says. What's rational about that morgue? Stained glass in the top halves of the windows, horrible glaring reds and greens.

Well—not my thing. No, creepy. Really, genuinely creepy. Gran? Supposed to be so clever. Gone into idiot mode if you ask me.

She swings round the corner and there, half way down to the next bend, is Nutmeg with his head over the gate blowing through his nose to greet her.

She feels his mealy nuzzle soft on her hand, slides her hand forward onto his smooth neck, rubs it, feels warmth rising under his mane, holds one apple to him in the flat of her hand, 'There you are, boy, there you are,' slips the halter over his head.

All the way back to the stable she holds her apple in her left hand, chewing as she goes, feels his warmth moving beside her, his head rising and falling as his feet go forward, smells something that once made her think of nutmeg.

At that time Mum had to lift me so I could get her hand on his withers. Now my legs have pushed my head so far from the ground I can see right over. Five eight and still growing. Mum thinks I'll end up a beanpole like Aunt Peggy.

His hooves make almost no sound in the soft dust. Leaves and sunshine are completely still. There's something in all this—in the stillness of trees, shadows, pools of sunlight—that lets you know the world has always been like this, a kind of sense of eternity, you and the pony the only things moving through it.

Less than a year ago it was that field in Fairhurst. All of them coming by the field path Jade, Carly, Shaz, Debs, Kev —did Kev ever come? All of them. It was good then before they dropped me. I'd been to all their houses. Didn't want to know—Carly—Jade—Debs—Kev. After I went to St. Anne's.

Clouds of dust fly as she leans her weight into the brush breaking up the last piece of caked mud on Nutmeg's hock, watching his coat begin to shine.

A rattle behind he makes her turn, 'Hiya, Shaz.'

'Hiya, Jo.' Shaz leans the bicycle against the wall, takes a quick glance, disappears into the stable, re-appears carrying saddle and bridle.

'Ta.'

'How's things then?'

'Not so bad. How they with you?'

'Talk about it later. Get on quick now.'

Jo hesitates, then smiles. 'Gran. Yeah.'

Soon Shaz is settling the saddle on the pony's back. Jo tightens the girths. 'You first. I'd fancy a go on your bike.'

Shaz and Nutmeg set off back down the green lane. Good seat, Shaz has. Natural. Sits into the pony's movement, straight, slim backed, straight brown hair swaying round her neck.

Nice bike too. Six gears. Shaz got it for her last birthday. Present from her Dad. Tough for him on his wages, my Mum said. Nice to be following down this lane with its surface of soft grit and the shadows of the hazels falling across it. Cool then warm, cool, then warm.

Shaz clucks to Nutmeg and touches him with her heels, rises to the trot, Jo still holding behind, so slow she can hardly keep the machine upright.

Old Ma Brown with her hand on a shoulder of each of us, pushing us gently. Her murmuring voice, *Sharon, sit at this table. Now you, Joanne, next to her.* First day at Primary school. Both five years old.

Where the lane divides and one branch swings away uphill onto the Downs, they exchange mounts. Nutmeg swings his head to greet her as she mounts. Jo settles into the saddle, gathers the reins. So familiar, this smooth leather under her thighs, the twists and turns of this lane, five-barred gate at the top with its handle adapted for riders to reach, open grass ahead.

Nutmeg seems pleased to extend himself across it, carrying her first, then Shaz. Then it's time to dismount at the summit and sit on the grass in the sun, Nutmeg tearing at it close by, the reins hanging on his neck. He won't go far.

They lie back side by side, their hands behind their heads. Not far away a grasshopper's scraping out its non-tune. Jo stares up at a small cloud. 'Seen Jade, then?'

'Don't want to know me nowadays.'

'What's wrong with her?'

'School. Don't suit her.' Shaz pauses, her voice deepens. 'She's limited, you know.'

'Kept up with us at St. Michael's.'

'Yeah, well. What she wants. By the way Kev's got a Mohican'

'Didn't the school throw a fit?'

Shaz laughs. 'Actually that guy's showing some sense.'

'That wally?'

'Got what it takes to brush out the colour weekdays,' she murmurs. 'Should see him week-ends.'

'Not likely to have the chance, am I?'

'I don't go round their place any more either, you know. Jade made it quite plain how boring I am. Swot, teacher's pet, you know the form.'

Her and Carly, putting their heads together, giggling, looking at me. *Come slumming, have you?* 'Jealous. Mum says. But why, Shaz? They think they know the world—so why be jealous of us?'

'Forget them.'

'Yeah.' She drops her head fully back on the grass, shuts her eyes. Red and blue flicker and flash behind the lids. She opens them again. 'D'you think they do know the world, really, better than us?'

'Just think they do. Want to have boys looking—'

'Yeah,' Jo says slowly, closing her eyes, stretching.

Shaz jerks up, gathers her knees in her arms, looks over them, shakes heavy hair back from her face. 'Gotta tell you.'

'What?' Jo says eyes still closed.

'Listen, can't you?'

Jo raises her head. The skin on Shaz's face is always too rough for her to be pretty. Just now she looks twenty-five. '

'My mum says it's time I bought my own clothes.'

Joanne rolls onto her elbow. 'So?'

'Got to pay for them, haven't I?' She pauses, takes a deep breath. 'Got a Saturday job.' She looks away, pulls at the grass. 'Starting next week.'

'So?'

'You thick or something? Means I can't come here.'

'But—Shaz—'

'Time I grew out of it, Mum says. People like us don't have ponies, she says. And I gotta have clothes.'

'Yeah, course, but—long as you have the basics.' Jo looks her friend over slowly. 'Don't need quantities.' She takes in tints she's never noticed before. 'What you been doing to your hair?'

'Highlights.'

'Yeah. Of course.' Lots of girls do at St. Anne's. 'We always been friends.'

'Still are. For goodness sake, still are.'

'Does it have to be Saturdays?'

'Look, Jo, my Mum's slaved all her life and where's she ended up? On the check-out in Tesco's. Great isn't it? Best she could do from where she started.' She plucks at the grass again, speaks without looking up. 'Not my idea of how to get on. I got to slog. Nothing won't come easy. School—plus Saturday job if I want some decent gear. Finish my homework first thing Saturday—then off to Newbold's Nurseries.'

'What you know about plants?'

'Not in the greenhouses. On the till same us my Mum—except I'm not going to stick there. Get some experience. Good on a CV. Shall pick up some names at least.'

'Always got to be learning, don't you?'

Shaz thumps the ground. 'If it were you—'

'Not, is it?' Her turn to pull the grass.

'Going to be a vet, aren't you? Or is that all talk?'

'Still time.' She leans towards her friend. 'For god's sake, what's the matter with you? You sound like my mum. Life's for living, you know.' She tries to catch her eyes but Shaz is avoiding. 'Maybe next year—but that's ages away—get O-levels over first. School's not everything. For god's sake' she says again, leaning on the words, 'don't let it take you over. Can always fit things round it—if you really want to'

'That what you think?'

'If there's anything to you, yeah.' Nutmeg's hoof scrapes over dry ground. Her eyes drop. 'Didn't mean that, Shaz. Just you took me by surprise.'

'OK—just get real, can't you? It's not about clothes, not really. Though I do have to have a decent top for school. Take that on board, Jo. She wants me to buy my school uniform. Know what she says about my Dad? Not stupid, she says, never done much neither. Worked for the Council thirty-five years. God, Jo, just think—thirty-five years slogging his guts out for the Council and no-one to thank him. Not much money neither. Could've done so much, she says. If only he'd bothered. So—him and her, you see, both of them—Not me. Going to bother all I can. Got it?'

'Get together, shall we? Sunday afternoons? I could come to your place.' She freezes, staring at the grassheads. 'If your Mum'll have me, that is.'

'No problem. Don't be a wally. All the same—not every week. My auntie comes and it's all family. What my mum wants.'

'Yeah. And I've got a Gran.' She rests in silence. 'Keep in touch, will we?'

Shaz nods.

Jo leaps to her feet. 'You have Nutmeg all the way back.' She seizes the bicycle, throws her leg over.

Shaz moves slowly towards Nutmeg, reaches for the bridle. 'Mind waiting?' She mounts, turns Nutmeg's head back towards the grassy summit, digs in her heels.

Jo drops the bike, watches as they disappear over the summit.

They reappear at a gentle canter which Shaz eases to a trot before turning his head back to the open space, digging her heels in, circling in a canter, tightening bent elbows, pulling him gently to a standstill. She jumps off. 'All yours now.'

Jo reaches out to the bridle. 'Sure?'

Shaz launches the bike with a kick, gives it its head the rough track rattling and bouncing downhill. Jo follows slowly.

Shaz waits in the shade of the hazels where the lane flattens out under the riding school hedge. At the sound of Nutmeg's hooves, a bright chestnut and a shaggy bay raise their heads whickering. He snorts, they come trotting down to keep pace with him the other side of the hedge. When rails take over from hawthorn, Jo lets him slacken.

At the top of the field Daphne Flack's unbridling a rangy grey. She raises an arm in greeting, slaps the horse's neck, strides down the field, the bridle swinging over her arm. 'Morning, Jo.'

'Good morning, Mrs. Flack.'

The two ponies are nuzzling her. Gently but firmly she pushes them away, 'You're out early.'

'Mum's taking me to visit Gran. Her birthday.'

'So how old's she then? Eighty, I reckon, if she's a year.' She nods, her eyes gleam. 'Tough old bird.'

Jo looks at her slowly. 'Yeah.'

'Can't spend all day standing talking to you. Though it's nice to see you. Jo.' She turns and turns back. 'Nice pony that. Don't forget. Offer's still open.'

'Yes, Mrs. Flack.' She watches a head of tight curls, a tight bottom in worn, well-cut jodhpurs, a pair of sturdy legs stride away back up towards the stable, lays her hand on Nutmeg's neck.

That stables over at Ranningham. He turned in his stall, leant his head over the door, wanted to see me.

That tough woman spoke over my head. *Exmoor.*

Pure-bred? Mum in let's-check-it-out mode.

Obviously some of that blood in him. They're calm, you know. Utterly reliable.

I reached up, took a first touch on that soft nose. *Let's call him Nutmeg.*

Haven't decided to buy him yet.

He's the colour of nutmeg. Red American cloth on the kitchen table, Mum rubbing a soft brown nut up and down against the grater, tiny curls piling onto junket—*Not its actual colour that it looks like—the colour of its smell.* Remember saying that, silly way of putting it but kind of not daft.

'What's she want, then?' Shaz asks.

'Buy Nutmeg. Thought I'd told you.' She'd said, *Nice pony,* as if you could put money on him.

'You were so sure you'd never think of it. Why I forgot.'

Jo shrugs, 'OK.'

The track runs softly now in the shadow of the hill, drowns their footsteps.

At length they reach the tarred lane, the entrance to Holmbush drive, the stables. Jo dismounts and turns to Shaz. 'You mustn't give up riding. You're a natural.'

'Things come to an end.'

'Not this. You can't just give up just because you want some kind of fancy gear. Thought you had more sense. You're not some kind of clothes horse. No-one is. Agreed that, didn't we?' In a dusty lair under the hedge at the end of the playground.

'Grow up, will you?'

'Thought you were really were my friend. Not though, are you? No better than the rest.'

Shaz flings her leg over her machine and swooshes off.

7.20 a.m.

Kate's been awake some time watching sunlight shift the window-bars across the ceiling. The angles sharpen and brightness gets tilted. John continues to breathe steadily; she eases herself upright against the pillow and the tip of the cypress rises above the sill, a dark point cutting across a blue that contains one small cloud. It's going to be a perfectly lovely day, just right for a go at the border under the bottom hedge—before the creeping thistle takes hold —but no, not today. Today's Mummy's day. Keep it special.

Her eyes slide past the clock on the bedside table—John to be got off to the golf course, Sheila coming—to wander over the wall, sprigs of honeysuckle scattered across it, almost at random it seems, natural and easy, so real—the shape of them, look, scent must be pouring out. And sometimes there's a temptation, sort of itching finger, wanting to put itself down on an edge where pink turns into yellow. No such place.

Everywhere used to be white paint, white wallpaper. *Clarity before all things.* Sun went in, it all went dead. S*teady north light.* Mummy woke up to the other side of house—this was only the spare room—but here first thing with sunlight coming in and a view if not of the garden at least of tree-tops, has to be better? At Back Lane trees all round the house, to be seen from all the rooms. Good years there, very good, seemed a beginning. Born here, began there. Born twice?

Or a long, slow birth? Beginning years ago, long before Back Lane, in that crowded kitchen—Sheila, her parents and that shining white castle on the table—though two slices already out—but her mother standing on a stool to reach into the top cupboard, *Let's see what we can find.*

Candles. *You light them, Kate.* Hand shaking, then the kitchen flickering, a ring of softly smiling faces.

Long lines of that squawking jab through the door. How can anyone call a wail like that music? Can't say anything to Jo, except, quietly, *Not before your Dad's up,* and hope. Try saying it again, more firmly. The voice has this tinny edge, almost a creak, as if someone's opening a door in a derelict house and there are things on the other side.

John doesn't stir. The back of his neck looks very strokeable—even though plumper than it used to be, bit redder too, but still those two folds running across under the ends of his hair—which he's not yet losing, still the same something that makes the nape of his neck so sweet. His breath's steady. All the same—Jo ought to think. Quite right to get up early—she's neglecting that pony. Told her to be back by ten but will she?

Get John's breakfast, Jo down to her homework and then calm to visit her Gran. Casserole for this evening. Should be finished by time Sheila arrives. *Pop in on my way to Earlhampton.* That voice after so many years. *Oh Sheila, it's you.* Gasping. *Not much time but....*

Once masses of time. Left with Mrs Forster, four, five years old perhaps. Warm back kitchen. Talk, talk, talk, Mrs Forster often out to the trains so mostly with Sheila—her mother's voice on the platform, *Change at Fairhurst for Earlhampton* and Sheila singing. What? Nursery rhymes? At first, possibly. Over the years always, always singing. Does she still? Could she ever not? *Teddy bears' picnic.* Picked it up first go from the wireless. *Somewhere over the rainbow.*

Kate glances at John's closed eyes, samples a few notes from something she should know well, *Once in royal David's city*. But Sheila's the one with the lovely voice, the one who got to High School and today's just dropping in. This friend she's going to visit Earlhampton, where'd they meet? Not that it matters. Why should it matter? Yesterday a voice on the phone, deeper, *Lovely to see you,* recognisable after a moment, those soft low notes, *And there for me, the apple tree* —their Newton Wonder that every year produced all those loads of apples.

And when Sheila's gone? What to do then? Jo should be back. But if not? Patience is golden. Read new syllabus? *Food Technology?* Instead of *Cookery*? Oh hell.

On the floor above a door opens, shuts, that little bit furtively. Feet pound downstairs. Jo hasn't got what it takes to deceive.

John still doesn't move. Kate flaps out her ears. Jo's in the kitchen now. The cake. Won't touch it, will she?

Ah—that's the back door so she's off out to that pony. Sit on it legs almost touching the ground. Get Pete to cut back the brambles. None the size of that monster at the corner of Back Lane. Johnsons cut it back. Where did Jo get those long legs from? Aunt Peggy? She was really tall—not a bean-pole—clothes flowed over her in the most terrifyingly elegant way. How to handle it if Jo turns out elegant? Any hope she'll be back for breakfast? She slips out from poly-cotton non-iron sheets—not as soft as pure cotton but easier to keep and so much better than drip-dry, which did drip and dry but crinkles never pulled out way the blah said they would—stands looking down on John. Still asleep. Get on with it. On top of everything else, Sheila. Lovely to see her, of course.

She hesitates on the landing, turns downstairs to the kitchen, smiles into the sun as she opens the door, turns out of it toward the dresser. Old Flowery used to park her bottom against that edge, arms folded, small pink mouth, layers of soft chin. *Our little miss.....*

Now, the cake. She whisks off the cloth. White icing still unblemished; 'Happy birthday' couldn't be neater. Not a bad job, not at all. Did well with those violets Five petals. Mummy sure to notice so checked. Something about five petals gets her excited. Maths in nature? *Whadyaknow?* Where'd that come from? How many years since—? Colour's exactly right, three drops of clear blue into wet icing, then, carefully, carefully, cochineal, tiny splashes and the shade changed. Odd—the shade they call violet not the colour of garden flowers, deep, rich, hiding under leaves but the faded in-between of plants growing in the open in shallow ground. Dog violets. Why dog?

A ring of eight and not roses. Not *ordinary*. Mummy looking, not stiffening her face, her birthday recognised after all these years. Said she didn't want so we never did. But. Underneath. Always want someone to notice. Only human. Mightn't have believed it once. Have proof now.

She drops the cloth lightly back, selects the mat with forget-me-nots, places it at the end of the table facing the window, collects spoon, knife, marmalade spoon, lays them beside it, easing each with the tips of her fingers into a position that feels right, pauses to breathe in sunlight that's warming her kitchen. It sparkles off clean cutlery, makes the day seem good. Which it will be, obviously. She lays out a cup and saucer, small bowl, corn flakes, Old Mill muesli, butter, marmalade, mat for the percolator. There, that's all ready for John. Been carrying the firm for years. And now—Senior Partner—look better after a day's golf. Eat her breakfast on the trot.

She slips on her apron, swallows a mug of tea, lays on the table one onion, three large carrots, a bag of stewing steak, selects a sharp knife, gets down to chopping, beginning to wonder if she was right to leave so much for this morning, sinking quickly into this familiar rhythm, looking forward to the scent of frying onions.

By 9.45. John's had his breakfast, been supplied with a flask. She's found his handkerchief, assured him she and Jo will be back before he is—not much after 5.30 even if Miss McDonald keeps them talking—promised to gives his best wishes to Mummy. The casserole's in the slow-cooker. She turns towards the sink. At no 16 window behind the sink looked over the lawn to the swing John put up for Jo's fifth.

And now she's leaning with her hands in the bowl looking over it into the garden, her view blocked by a brick wall, not picturing anything though turn left to the top terrace and from there an invisible ray draws across the valley, over Steadings farm and the woods beyond, lifts over the hill to sink down through Ashmead, converge on the line of the railway where Station House is, converted now but Sheila's coming today. Why on earth? Day of Mummy's party. *Brian off at a conference so I've time,* so *Of course, do come.* But—

Running her own business. Always in her? Didn't occur to anyone. Went into the bank—and then—

Any other day—more time—but all the same—Sheila.

Beside her years ago watching trains; chuff, chuff and off; Ashmead Halt, Fairhurst.

Yes, Fairhurst.

Out of sight from here. First day, with John. Came on the bus. Got off at the Bull—pub-crawler bus, stops one after another. Ship, Royal Oak, Bull, Lace-makers' arms. Walk Main Road into Hebden Road into Back Lane. *End terrace, extensive garden.* John's warm hand.

Bramble at the corner all over the place. Village so down-market after Gilbridge. But nice. Bungalow on the corner with hanging baskets, really good feel to it. Backs of Main Road houses on the left, fences, ends of sheds, bit rough looking, but OK, not sordid; right side better, the Smiths' villa, the Westons', then the privet hedge, its top all up and down because each owner trims it a different height; the Williams' laburnum, the Bridgers' red-leaved plum. Elm terrific at the end, after that only a cart track down to Field End Farm.

Last on the right, wooden gate with a top rail just the right height to lay a hand on. Petals from the Victoria across herringbone brick, not the gooey mess of wet years, but lightly scattered, still pure white. It had been a dry spring.

The owner will show you round.

Yes, but *What shall we say?*

John's hand pushing gently forward.

How'll we know if we like it? Sun on white paint. Gleaming brass knocker.

John drawing close sliding out an arm, the sleeve of his rough jacket pressing down, warm, scratchy—shabby tweed with leather patches on the elbows that he went on wearing years after everyone else. His hand on the knocker, the way it rang out.

After the washing up she devotes herself to the top of the Aga: dab on Jif with a soft cloth, rub slowly, firmly, see brown spots fade, the whole thing shine up clean, hygienic; take time, learn to be pleased with what you've done. What they said at the Institute. Repeated to 4E this year, 4B last year and will go on being repeating it right up till retirement presumably.

The icing points are still where she left them to dry, one round no 2, one flat no 104. She picks them up in her finger-tips, fits them into their box beside an icing bag that won't let her wash out cochineal stains, shuts them all in, slips the box into the left side of the third drawer.

Now for the cake.

She gets down the carton, spreads the strip of folded white cloth on the dresser beside it, slides her fingers under the cake-board, transfers her casket onto the cloth, lifts the two ends—perhaps getting it out ask Jo to take one?—lowers it all gently, drops the ends beside the cake, reaches for the packet containing eight candles—eighty's beyond limits—surely Mummy wouldn't insist on that—or would she?—can eight stand for eighty? How can anyone ever make out what she wants?

Puzzling that day—that man beside her, some kind of big-wig, and that knife in her hand, her giving a cake such a concentrated, almost tender look? Best tweed suit, brown lace-ups, headmistress kind of style—Speech Day but not so dressy—dressy for her—

Matches. She rifles through the small left-hand drawer, pulls out a box, opens it, does a rough count—you can't always rely on the first. Her eyes narrow. Jo—it'll have to be Jo that lights them—will guide the flame across the cake; its light will soften her face, showing the child still there under the teenager. Must get her to hold back her hair. Mummy will watch? With what expression? Look away? Or that vague look?

Not vague. Not vague, no, just that old people tend to be dreamy.

This man with her whoever he was. Name must've been announced sometime. Standing behind the table, presenting Mummy with this knife. And her smiling, accepting it, sort of measuring the icing with her eyes, pointing the tip down so neatly, so carefully and sliding it into the exact centre. Everyone standing about clutching their teas. Had been shouting at each other till a series of loud raps. *Now Mrs. Lomas...*

Get down to that syllabus. Ugh, She pushes the chairs into place, straightens them parallel with the table. Mrs. Forster's table had soft, rounded edges. Scrubbed every day, whitened. That place in Gilbridge for Mummy—that dark wood after all those white walls?

The clock's hands are moving relentlessly on. Can't stop it. Nothing to do but wait. Jo, Sheila, Mummy. She pulls out a chair, sinks onto it. That syllabus. One finger starts up, rapping the table, tap-tap-tap—tap-tap. That girl, dawdling all this time, not eating a proper breakfast.

Young enough to get away with it. And she will come in. Eventually. The finger stops in mid-tap, her lips soften. What it is to have a daughter, *For god's sake, Mum, mind those pins. Stand still then,* and the scatterbrain jumps again. Later, on the phone, *You should see it, Shaz, totally brill. My Mum's a genius.*

But Mummy? *A very unhappy woman?* Who said that? Mrs Forster? Last Thursday perhaps looking up from her chair in that small front-room? What she says—nowadays—old. Caught up in past. Though why? Mummy always clear, definite. Knew what she wanted. No doubt, wrist grabbed, pulled down beside her to squat on the floor, four years old maybe. *Triangles, squares, circles. Look Kate,* her finger running across the carpet. *Use your eyes. You can count can't you, up to four? Here in the pattern, look.* And finally, *Surely to goodness—* that finger darting along red lines and blue lines which kept bending like broken twigs and getting mixed up, snakes with broken backs all tangled together. She'd snort, draw these shapes on bits of paper. *Look, Kate, look.* Stare, stare. Lines, thin, faint pencil lines. Put them together, make stick-men—horrible hard shapes, making fun of people. Skeletons. In life shapes always come roughed up in bodies or in brown wood or red bricks, parts of things—table-tops —and it's the table that matters—yes you do have to think if there's room for it and where it'll stand and round and square suit different rooms—that round table we had in Back Lane just wouldn't fit here—very sad but that's life and when a fish's being filleted the bones aren't what's wanted but the flesh; poach it slowly in milk with onion and a bay-leaf and serve it with new potatoes and carrots or peas to make a contrast of colour; they'll smell wonderful and look good on the plate and the pieces will have a good texture.

Every time she went on and on about triangles and squares —no brain for any of this, only tears that would keep escaping. No hope, ever, and at last—at last she saw—her daughter, who should've been so clever, couldn't help being plain stupid. In the end, at last, she gave up.

When's Jo coming? *My Mum's a genius.* Dressmaking always a joy, easing material to fit, gently stretching the curve of an arm-hole or collar.

Sun rests on the draining board. White tiles reflect the cooker, the light hanging stationary over the table on the end of its long flex, herself as she gazes round. Tomatoes, peppers, carrots, painted but so realistic, hang like a curtain across a window to a roomful of dim-edged shadows.

Something moves past the window. She lays down the matches, stands, lets a smile burst across her face. 'Come in,' and as the door opens, 'Oh Sheila, you've made it.'

2

10.25 a.m.

The kind of knock one can't be expected to hear announces the arrival of a man who ambles in grinning, clutching his bag of tools, quite at home apparently. Has one seen him before? 'Miss McDonald says fire needs looking at.'

Why should she say that? Who told her? Why the fire? It would be much better if he removed that object standing in the corner. She couldn't ask a man to handle that so she said the fire instead.

'Why are you seeing to the fire on Sunday?'

He pauses. 'It's Saturday, Mrs. Lomas.'

He looks at one the way people do. It is reasonable to wonder.

He pulls himself together, lumbers across the room, altering the shapes of objects as he passes, spreads a cloth in a rough rectangle that interrupts the patterns in the carpet, kneels, opens his bag, takes out a screwdriver, fits the tip into an invisible groove, turns. She watches intently as a small, bright object falls into the cup of his left hand. He shuffles sideways, repeats the procedure, lifts off a panel and lays it on the floor beside him at a slight angle to the cloth.

It fitted so exactly and then came off. Pale, plump fingers gripped something tiny and bright, a meaty wrist turned a small screwdriver. A man handling metal, lightly, precisely.

Slim fingers push on a brownish tube, the other hand grips the stock, the sun shines as he breaks open the barrel and shows that dark hole. *D'you see—the rifling?* Deep, narrow darkness. *Try feeling.*

The tip follows the spiralling of some thin, raised hardness, till the whole finger's jammed in.

The wonder of metal, his voice is eager, *it can be made to fit so exactly, its proportions measured in fractions of a millimetre.* Slim fingers stroke the barrel of a Webley. *There has to be a mind behind these things.* Where have you sprung from, George?

Fingers and a gun—distant—though his voice is beside one—clear in themselves when one can hold them—one's peering through a gap between leaves. Why does he stand here talking when he's holding the gun over there, something more than those fingers—a grassy place, a building?

She closes her eyes. That way things sometimes come clearer. And for a minute they do.

That morning—11.30 perhaps—shadows comparatively short—in the centre of rough grass beside that ramshackle firing shed—he takes it out of the holster, slips the strap over his arm, handles grey steel. His slim fingers grip the stock. The other hand rests on the barrel. He looks up, holds it out. *Feel its weight.*

'Shouldn't give any more trouble.'

She opens her eyes with a start. A man in overalls is standing up now, dusting his knees and beyond him she catches up with a window, a blue curtain, bookshelves, a mahogany table, ends of something trailing off, drifting apart as one tries to grasp them.

He gives her a long look, a kindly smile. 'Be going then.'

'Thank you. Most kind.'

The name sitting in her mind seems right. Someone called himself George? One George, a king called George, two Georges?

A male voice announces, 'I'll let Miss McDonald know,' the door closes. She presses her hands together. One must be half asleep thinking rubbish like this. Good thing no-one else is in the room. And they're not because someone just went and that panel fits so exactly. Only an almost invisible line shows it's not an integral part of the fire-front.

The feel of a gun comes again now, lighter than one might have expected— the grip roughened in a subtle pattern of sloped and dotted diamonds—one traced it out with a finger-tip—easy to hold; it hangs freely at the end of the arm, a weight fitting the hand—sunlight glints on the barrel as one tilts it up, one's back to the sun. *A range faces north to avoid dazzle.* Instructing, endlessly instructing. She tightens her lips, rests back in her chair.

'Miss. Ingram.' A name called softly, almost sung to make it carry. 'Miss Ingram. Miss Ingram.' Feet hurry outside the door. 'Can I help you Miss Ingram?'

That mad woman again but in this room the panel fits exactly and Miss McDonald has at last taken away that object. She closes her eyes for a clearer view of a row of targets at the foot of a cliff. The place an old quarry, the ground soft with shed leaves but still enough left on the trees to muddle their framework. October. What day is it? It can't be Thursday.

He smirks when one has to ask, *What's that behind the targets?* fidgets when one takes the time necessary to inspect the wall of railway sleepers, weigh up how far they'll absorb the impact of stray bullets, examine the angle of inclination. *Forward to deflect them onto the ground. Like to see me shoot?* He disappears into the shed. The holster projects from the ledge under the firing window. *Come and stand here.*

He breaks open the rifle, inserts cartridges, click, click, click into the cylinder—till there are six. He firms it shut, stretches his right arm at full length, looking along the sights, lining them up, provides a splendid view of his profile. His cheeks glow.

Became gaunt later. When he became a boffin—six years away being a boffin. Six years away, big figure in a small back room.

Six rounds, six reverberations off the rock, six holes clustered close to the bull's eye. *Not bad at fifty yards.* He's smiling up into the soft October sun.

He offers the gun, laughing. *What about you having a try?* One takes it. His eyes widen. He leads the way back to the firing shed. *Now load it.*

And now her lips are firmed together in a tight smile. The barrel in one's left hand exactly like him, the palm held out flat, the way she's holding it now without thinking, reaching into the room. *Cartridges.*

You've done this before.

The cartridges, please. Slip them in, release with the first finger of the right hand allowing the cylinder to revolve, look straight at him.

You're an unusual girl.

Stretch the right arm the way he has, fix the eye on the sights, pull the trigger. Newton's Third Law comes to life violently against bones and muscles. Five more times.

Let's go and look at the results, shall we?

Four holes, only just below the centre of the target.

Clever girl, only two misses.

She reaches for her mohair rug. The sun's off her chair now but George is still lounging in the space at the foot of the old sleepers.

How far above the target should you aim?

He starts, palpably starts. *A bullet drops seven inches over fifty yards.*

One raises one's head. That's how one deals with him. *Its path a parabola.*

He hesitates and that says so much but one doesn't see it, *I'd forgotten you're Natasha's maths teacher.* He chuckles, *Treated you like a normal girl.*

She pulls the rug more closely round her, glaring at him. *Yes —I do teach your niece mathematics—or try to.*

Not much good, is she?

Average, as I said to Mrs. Ivings.

Peggy thought you were somewhat generous.

I always try to be accurate. And you shoot accurately.

His eyes run over one like rain. *Shall I show you again?*

If you like.

One stands there and lets him.

A car passes in Parsons Avenue, a windscreen wiper sweeps and the whole story's gone.

That's father's bureau. Those are one's own books, one's own curtains. That's a telephone ringing. The noise must emerge from a window on the ground floor, rise up outside and come in here.

A car rushes past, shaking those leaves there outside the window. And another.

Bushes arch over a track. At the edge of a rug, humped roots snake about exposed in the open. Between them patches of warm red soil. That's where the rug is. One leans on the right hand, feels beechmast through thick wool, legs folded sideways, skirt pulled down over the ankles. Hiding lisle stockings? They're not Peggy's.

Car parked to the right, left side in the sun. Good clean metal lines—flat rectangular radiator, triangular shining top, two large, circular headlamps. Interesting contrast. George crows, *Morris Oxford Six.*

One murmurs, *Very satisfactory design;* he goes on boasting. *Took delivery six weeks ago.* His fingers move across a greaseproof packet, delicately picking apart folds. *Nice little job, don't you think? More power than the bullnose.*

Small triangular sandwiches, predictably chicken and it's cool here on the ground under the beech trees. Dappled shadow. George runs on and on. One's not judging the fact he's not found much to say, simply letting the mind rest on that moment when one planted the feet, stretched the arm forward, six shocks ran up it, shots reverberated from the rocks. Listen, one, two three, they shake the walls between the bookshelves.

Will they leave marks? What will Miss McDonald say?

He pauses at last. One must acknowledge his efforts. *Thank you for this morning. I learnt so much.*

Not a woman's thing, eh?

Could you show the flight-path on graph paper?

That catches his attention. *D'you mean that?*

Of course. Velocity over distance—

He considers this strange specimen slowly from head to toe and back, decides the effort's worth it, pushes himself to his feet, walks quietly to the car, returns swinging the holster. He pulls out the gun. *I'll show you something you won't have seen.* Smug eyes gleam.

He breaks open the barrel, holds it out. *Look down that.*

His breath warmer, closer. *Put your finger in. Can you feel the rifling?*

The what? Some narrow projection from the wall, apparently regular.

Ridges spiralling down inside the barrel. Know what they're for? He's not waiting for a fuzzy little head to come up with the answer. *They put a spin on the bullet that exerts a centripetal force that helps to hold it on course when it leaves the muzzle.*

The familiar algorithms in action. His face even closer. *You're an interesting girl.*

Help me up, will you? One's obliged to hold out a hand. His fingers warm, pressing.

All those outings, so many of them, such lovely weather, riversides, hills, tea-shops ....

Her breathing becomes heavier.

10.25 a.m.

Nutmeg stamps and shakes his halter. She stands back. His coat's shabby. Mane God-awful. 'I wouldn't ever let you go. Know that, don't you?' His head turns. She places her hand both sides of his neck, leans towards his soft nose. 'Oh Nutmeg, I've got to waste my afternoon in that horrible house.' That isn't all that it is. The day's gone black. It's full of emptiness and darkness. 'You're so lucky you don't have to go there. It's night in the middle of the day and this horrible old woman creeping about.' Like what Jade said years ago, *That old witch next door. Mum says she oughta be put down. Off her rocker.* This one—not witch—*You should respect her.* Yeah yeah but. Creeping about, going on how she wants to go to Andover.

Andover where's that? Andover—Endover. One of those book jokes—Shaz and me up—year we had 'Jones the Beard'—no sense of humour him—'Cliff tragedy by Eileen Dover.' Tell Shaz. Uncontrollable giggles pound through her till she remembers and the emptiness swallows her.

Eyelids fringed by pale hairs make mounds each side of his long nose. She glances up at the sun.

Later she strokes his nose. 'Shouldn't have been laughing, Nutmeg. You wouldn't have laughed, would you? Old lady can't help it.' But she's not the worst of it even with torn cobwebs all round her head. Call that hair? 'Comes just because someone's opened the front door, just to tell you she wants to go to Andover.'

Her arms drop. 'Gran not much fun either. I have to sit there while she keeps forgetting. Face goes all vague, no light in it. Mum says she doesn't but she does. Not imagining it, am I? What is it with old people, Nutmeg? Why can't they keep themselves on track? Keep their brains active, not so difficult, is it? When I get to their age, I won't let myself go like that.' She buries her face again in his mane. 'Won't, will I? What do you think?'

First his feet. She works round, raises one after the other, jerks out nodules of caked mud. Dust spurts over her. She places the last back on the ground; the pony nuzzles her arm; she straightens, dashes straggling hair back out of her eyes, discovers her cheeks are wet. 'Oh Nutmeg, I'm so sorry. So sorry.'

She sets to work on his fetlocks with the curry-comb. It's been dry lately so they're not too bad. Slowly she works up his legs, reaches into the soft places of his tummy and he stands and as she moves up over the rounds of his haunches, reaches up to his crupper and then along the long line of his spine—so easy now to reach across—she feels his sides relax under the brush, the air full of his soft breath.

She changes to the soft brush, sweeping her arm in big circles across his flanks, breathing heavily herself by this time, leaning her weight into the movement and sees a shine rising through his coat. Soft, light bay. Then it's his head, his ears, his long nose, the Exmoor's mealy muzzle.

She wants to throw he arms round his neck again but holds back. She's not a kid. Strange though how an animal can be a better friend than another human. Proves you don't need to talk—though something like language is going on between them, The two of them together here in this stable, in the shadowy light, the sunshine a brilliance outside reaching in through the door as a sharp-edged triangle.

No sound—no blackbird, insistent starling, none of the crows that nest in the holm oak. Mum hasn't decided to come looking. Just Nutmeg and me. Friends.

She rests a hand on his neck. The whole problem in every way is school.

Basically that's Gran's fault.

'Oh Nutmeg, you've always been so smart. Not fair to take it out on you.'

She arranges the brushes in their box, pushing each one delicately with her finger-tips to make sure its bristles lie straight, taking in how comfortable they look together. goes back to the pony, rests her hand on his neck looking out through the open door into the yard, not consciously observing how the shadow's shifted since they came in.

At last she unhitches the halter from the end of the stall, leads him out; the strike of his hooves softens as they enter the track towards his field.

The sun's higher now, almost overhead, the shadow from bushes leaning together is deeper. Small creatures that were busy earlier have disappeared. As she enters the wood the sound of voices and a soft padding meets her from somewhere ahead. She peers through the branches. There they are, fragments of chestnut and bay, four or five of them probably, with riders in grey and cream. She draws Nutmeg aside onto the fallen beech leaves.

The ponies emerge one by one round the bend in the path. Nutmeg stretches his head towards them and blows through his nose and the ponies nicker back. She stands taking them in. That first girl's got a good seat, She raises a hand, 'Hi,' and they answer, 'Hi there.' Daphne's on that grey she's always on about—how great he is—and he does hold himself well—third in the party, leading a small kid on a Shetland.

'We meet again, Jo.'

'Yes, Mrs. Flack.' And Nutmeg blows again through his nose, reaching it out as the horses come close, while Jo scans the riders. About her age In very swish jodhs—Emma something or other. Don't know that red-head; kid on the Shetland lives in that big red house near the bus stop? Seen her or another like her—coming home from school. Rest of them? Don't know, don't care. Casuals. Same pony gives rides to dozens every week.

Together she and Nutmeg watch till the last tail swishes off round the corner. Then she tugs at his head, 'Come up, boy.' Briefly he digs in his feet, then yields and follows, head hanging, hooves tittupping on stony sand.

They reach the field, she removes the halter. pats his neck, gives him a soft slap on the rump as he turns away, lowers his head starts grazing. She leans on the gate. He gradually drifts forward away from her.

She lowers her chin onto her hands. The sun's warm on her shoulders but the air round here is unsatisfactory. Difficult to know why—there's a blackbird there, row of black bodies dangling from its beak, must have a nest not far off, busy, trees all round, sweet chestnut, hazel, oak, the hawthorn hedge, standing there calm in the sun, stretching out their branches, enjoying themselves, absorbed in their own lives, leaving her out, in the centre of a hole, a great white emptiness. It's not like when she's wandered down the garden to hide and get away from them all and sat there under a bush listening, knowing Dad's at work, Mum's in the kitchen and she's free, doesn't really need to hide but it's fun, they seem miles away and she's run off into her own life. This emptiness isn't like that. It's cold, full of separation. She's never felt so alone before, standing here isolated.

Mum's probably working herself into a tiz in the kitchen over Gran and that stupid cake and the time, Dad's off to his golf, Shaz—and Shaz—

Other 'friends'—girls at school—well they are friends—but not like Shaz. Wendy's gone shopping with her Mum, Maggie's out with her boyfriend—rest of them—who knows? Miles away, they'll tell me all about it on Monday, the great time they've had—getting on with their own lives, full of themselves as if that's what I most want to hear, all about them, not caring. Come down to it, do I care what they got up to? Does anyone really really care what anyone else gets up to?

This what it's really like? Tiny creature living in an enormous hole with everyone else outside. Always like that? Always this loneliness?

She looks at something too real to cry over, something that takes you by the shoulders and says, stand up, get on with it. You're on your own now. She pushes herself off the gate, starts stumping back towards the house.

10.37 a.m.

The sun-backed blur in the doorway—is a chicken—that's rude—oldest friend—must still be one—call her a hen? Even if slim, tall breed, Leghorn perhaps, but all the same, the shape widening from the top of the head, flowing down, hair like feathers gleaming over the shoulders, comfortable look lower down, not that plump but somehow an air of a mother—take charge, that was her—

and then the narrowness of legs, weight more on one than the other, one hip tilted way she always did, looking round, and it's not that baleful glare a hen gives you but a clear glance, turning her head, her chin levelled the way it would be, eyes tight at the corners. Has an air. Used to giving orders. She'll have staff. Middle aged. Does that mean—? Obviously Kate, think—time—

Look at her face now. Bones underneath don't alter. What passport officers look for. Waiting to come into this kitchen, 'Come in. Come on in,' but it's different. When you've thought about someone so often—though she only rang yesterday—and then they're here, solid, taking up space, radiating across the air. What are her thoughts? There's an aura round her—faint cream walls, brown paint, a stove, shiny American cloth, two small girls clasping fat wax crayons, showing each other drawings. Station House. Where else?

'Come on in. Sit down.' Here, on a bright morning like this, surely everything must be gleaming back at her, ordinary sensible things but nice, blue and white plates along the dresser, blue and white cups above them on hooks, Kilner jars in glass-fronted cupboard, white wall-tiles scattered at random with realistic tomatoes, peppers, carrots so it all looks natural.

Firm lips stretch into a smile that's more Sheila and deserves a welcome which is being delayed. Kate rushes to the coffee machine, begins to measure quantities in a small brown plastic cup, turns back to take in the presence there in the doorway, light slanting across fair hair that lies more smoothly than it used to.

'Like the real thing, don't you?' But she's still gazing. 'This room's so peaceful now, Kate.'

Two kids then, backs resting against the hot pipes from the Cook-an'-Heat, frozen into not fidgeting while Mummy poked a pot of potatoes. Today a swing of the arm, dramatic but anything to get her moving. 'Come on then, right in.'

Sling-back sandals clack across quarry tiles, Sheila pulls out a chair. 'Seems to me it was always a bit glum.' She still doesn't sit. 'Could have been wrong, I suppose.'

'Did it?' Here's the water coming through now. What a rush of brown bubble and plunge. 'Do make yourself comfortable. Suppose it wasn't exactly Mummy's favourite room.' The one she never got painted white. Neglected. Give it a minute or two longer. 'Cooking's never been her thing.' There it is, full scented coffee, ready at last. 'Two thirds full, I seem to remember?' She pours carefully. 'Got a bit dingy, perhaps.'

Sheila subsides onto the chair. 'Mrs Flowers wasn't that fussy.'

'You can say that again. Mummy had to have her.'

'You've made it so nice.'

Kate bends towards her friend and sees Mr Forster—though she hasn't thought of him for years, not to picture him. Sheila's face is still squarer than her father's, his was more narrow, but the same bones. And he was a man of course, so the skin's smoother. He was so much on the platform. All that open sky. Once you come out of the woods, level with the beginning of the embankment, such a lot of sky. Five trains a day, and the two carriage 'Illington Flyer' with its engine on backwards that went down to the paper mill morning and evening to fetch the workers.

'You put in the milk for yourself.' She retreats to the dresser and looks back. Her hair, that's it. Used to be tumbly like her mother's. Hangs straight now, help of a good hairdresser, emphases the firm lines. 'No option, not hygienic, walls had to be dealt with.' She picks up a plate of small cakes each crowned with a glacé cherry. 'Haven't really changed anything.'

Sheila's eyes swing towards the Aga.

'That was Daddy. Persuaded her to get rid of that awful old Cook-an'-Heat. Remember it? All right in its day. But. Late Sixties. Oil the cheapest fuel. Before the Crisis, remember? Dresser's exactly the same, and the big wooden cupboard.'

Sheila leans back, brings her fingers together, seems to be taking her turn to probe a face. 'You said she's moved out?'

'What she wanted.' She settles herself at the opposite end of the table, smiles placatingly. 'Not sure I've got the cakes the way your mother did.' She goes on studying Sheila. Eventually her face brightens. 'D'you remember, your Dad caught us drawing a hopscotch on the platform?'

Their eyes rise sideways, converge and in the warmth of the ensuing giggle Kate continues, 'We were on out there so much. Did you miss it, moving away?' Buffers ringing out like bells as the push ran through them. Lying in bed quarter of a mile away, the music of shunting making a path through the woods. 'A station's all about going away—must accept that I suppose—but—did you miss it?'

'At first but you move on.'

'Remember how your mother used to shout the station names and her voice swooped up towards the end?' *Bagham, Illington Junction, Swailton Halt, Gilbridge*—to the great world beyond.

They chew slowly, each with one hand resting on the table, one finger touching warm earthenware. Then Kate takes a deep breath. 'She says you're setting up in Gilbridge.' Figure looking up from an armchair, so small now, seeming to shrink steadily week by week—and once upon a time she'd blow a whistle. An engine puffed and snorted, pulling its shoulders together like a cart-horse, moving off. She'd have planted her feet right down into the earth, right arm above her head waving the flag, the company cap perched on top of her curls. Always in that chair now. *It was my back let me down*—other bits later. Turning up her face, talking about her daughter, dimmed eyes swimming with pride.

Sheila leans back, drawing the sun over her. 'Haven't closed down in Sevenoaks yet. Got an excellent assistant so I've left her in charge. Shall need to borrow but a steady income's guaranteed there—so—'

The voice deepens, becomes firmer, but still the same. *When I take you out in the Rover*—Her in shiny tights and a sharp cut jacket waving an arm towards the Principal Girl. *The Rover with the flag on top.* Looking up at her from the third row in the High School hall, warm bulk of her mother beside you, clapping and clapping, *Encore, encore* and that clear voice again, *Think how all of Gilbridge will hover*—

They will, they will. Soon as she opens it. 'What you calling it?'

A Sense of Fashion.

Look at the square white collar on her blouse, the blue-green eye shadow. Oh for her style. She was always the brave one. 'Found anywhere yet?'

'Maybe.' She pauses, seems to be approaching something sideways 'Tell me, Kate, what d'you think of Mum?'

'Always seems cheerful—but then, she would.'

'Yes.'

'Be glad to have you within reach.'

'Yes.'

Coocoocoo drifts in, repeated over and over. Collared dove on the plum tree—or the kitchen roof and Sheila in that seersucker blouse with its yellow and soft orange checks with a fine green line running through them. Her hair her mother's smoothed down, her body slim like her father's. Wearing scent—could be Dior? Looking down at the table, saying nothing.

Her mother's overall. Boiled every week, pounded in quantities of bleach and soap, coarse cotton still discolouring, never really fresh, its sour smell mixing with the scent from the oven and Mrs Forster, bending from the hip, hand wrapped in a heavy cloth, drawing out a hot tin, placing it on a mat on the table. Where there'd been squidgy dough, this airy golden curve. Feeling her warm bulk, knowing she didn't think it was stupid to delight in this miracle.

Kate sparks to her feet. 'Now you're here. You wouldn't mind? Oh Sheila, it's wonderful having you here.' She trots to the dresser. 'A little lookie?'

Sheila tautens. Then smiles, rises to her feet. 'That box had to be something.'

Fiddling with the lid. 'I did violets. Think they're OK?'

'You've really got those petals.' She comes up beside her, leaving a small distance. 'Can't be easy to make them look soft. But they do, you've got them, Kate. And that lovely colour.'

Kate broods over the cake. 'Ordinary sort of blue straight out of the bottle isn't that strong so—just a weenie touch of pink. Not sure. Bit strange maybe? Off-key, somehow?' The emptiness that sometimes slides into Mummy's eyes? Doesn't, of course. Simply imagined. She gazes at her friend. 'What you think? And the spacing. Not quite, quite, perhaps?'

'What's all this then? Your mother come into it somehow?'

Kate raises her chin. 'Her eightieth birthday. Make a bit of a splash.'

Sheila touches her shoulder. 'But, Kate—'

'No harm getting things right,' she says pulling away.

Sheila takes herself back to the chair, looks up. 'Excellent coffee. Suppose there isn't any more going?'

While Kate rushes up with the flask, she sits tapping the table, watches her pour and when she's finished says gently, 'Went to special classes didn't you?'

'Yes.' She puts down the flask, feels warmth rush through her. Cycling through the dark to evening classes—City and Guilds Baking and Confectionery Part 1, and in successive years, Parts 2 and 3. Icing cakes not part of Olive Firman's vision for *instructing Working Class Mothers in The Principles of Good Nourishment,* even when updated for the Twentieth Century. Kate tucks the lid in round the cake.

Sheila fingers the mug, watching, and when she still doesn't sit, enquires casually, 'That a good place—in Gilbridge?'

Kate frowns, rubbing the worktop; then her face clears, she turns back to face Sheila who's sitting there all neat in the sunshine. 'Lots to say for it—Parsons Avenue among others, relatively quiet—but when she chose it—and she was the one chose it—we were all for her staying here—she got so angry—almost shouted at John.'

'She never used to shout.'

'Well, this time she did.' She returns to driving her finger backwards and forwards across the worktop as if ridges in vinyl are endlessly fascinating. 'Don't understand.' Eventually pivots on her elbow. 'Sorry, don't know why I'm pouring all this over you. Second time we've met in years and I'm going on.'

'Ageing parent. Natural to be upset. I know the syndrome.' Sheila smoothes her face into a shining blandness. 'But if she's happy where she is?' Coocoocoo drifts in again from the garden, a soft-centred mantra. 'And she does seem to be, does she?'

'Far as anyone can tell.'

'Well then?' Her voice has a sharp edge.

'As you say—well then—' That blasted dove. Endlessly, endlessly and never anything useful to say. 'Tell me, how's —Mark—is it? Sorry. Awful to forget but I'm rotten at names.'

And now a real smile surfaces. 'Mark, yes. Will die if he can't have a pair of Doc Martens by yesterday.' Eyes meet fully this time, the pair of them giggling like teenagers; the air gentle as the grey of a collared dove. Then Sheila, 'You know, Kate, I'd rather hoped to get a glimpse of Jo.' Two toddlers in baby-gros, sitting on the floor solemnly taking one another in. How many years ago?

'Not taking life as seriously as she should, otherwise fine.'

Sheila follows Kate's eyes to the clock. 'Going with you?'

'That's the idea.' Those hands have already moved on. 'Out with Sharon. The pair of them bucketing around on that pony. Not that I mind, nice girl, Sharon.' She raises her eyes shyly, 'Good friend for her—like you've been to me all these years.'

'Gone our different ways.' Is that in her voice—a touch of sadness?

Kate slowly returns to the table and sits, starts playing with a tea-spoon. 'By the time I came back you were going out with Brian.' Digging in the tip of the spoon. 'And earlier—'

'Should've made your mother let you try the 11+. You're not stupid.'

Kate shrugs, stares at the table The spoon hasn't left a mark. Her face eases. 'Might've felt I ought to teach in that kind of school. Better where I am. With ordinary kids.' She rubs again, then murmurs, still gazing at her fingers. 'Never told you did I? How could I? You weren't here. Made me think.'

Sheila plumps out her feathers and after a pause, 'Think what?'

'Don't know,' she informs the table. 'Well, I do of course.' She looks up and at last her fingers fall still while she searches Sheila's face. 'Basically, County are a load of bureaucrats who keep on the 11+ so they don't need to spend out on females who fail it.'

'Ye-es. So?'

'This do at County Hall, two years before Daddy died—no great cop, I thought at the time.' She firms herself up. 'Still don't.' And after a pause, 'Daddy was chairman of the shooting club for years and years. Some of them were councillors. How he got invited.'

'So?'

'Never occurred to me Mummy could have anything to do with this.'

'I'm sorry. You've lost me.'

'11+ and all that.'

'You knew she was on the Council? Surely? But Kate—what is this? She was at County Hall that day?'

'Been off out to meetings long as I knew. Which I thought was great—nip off down to your place.' She grins, blurts out, 'Never bothered what she was getting up to—' suddenly stares—'Did you know, then?'—and rushes on, 'Yes, she was.'

'Aha,' Sheila says softly.

Kate gives her a long glance, leans forward—'Ever seen inside County Hall?'—and grins at the head-shake. 'No reason you should have. If you do get the chance, don't, that's what I'd say, it'll only depress you.' Concrete; pillars, steps, hall, corridors, photos of moustachioed men who wouldn't ever have let a smile crack their faces. 'Not a soul to tell you which way to go. Daddy took off left. I tagged along behind'—through air compressed by blank walls —'and there suddenly round a corner was an assistant taking coats'—at a table in a dark corner beside double doors. 'Daddy barged ahead'—into that mob in suits, standing about with glasses, shouting at each other—'found some blokes he went shooting with and I was left not knowing a soul.'

'You would be. Oh Kate—'

At the far end, beyond the bodies, a long table, starched white cloth, glasses, cutlery. 'Got myself a glass of white and as it seemed nothing was going to happen sneaked a pre-view of the eats—see what ideas they'd had—you never know. Hadn't got much beyond finger-rolls and the cake no credit to professional caterers. Sort of dingy green-grey—shadow probably under the wall, you know, on the far side from the windows—but all the same royal icing hard as an ice rink. Seemed to me they'd need a hammer to get through. 'Bout as nice as a frozen hockey pitch. 'Hardshire County Council 1875-1975' across the top. White on white, can you credit it?'

Sheila shakes her head again, smiling.

'Then it all went quiet and this big-wig in a brown suit appeared on the platform.' She leans forward to gaze into Sheila's eyes. 'Mummy'd gone off earlier, on her own you know, I never asked where, so used to it—you know how it was—but you knew? And there she was up there beside him—Mrs Lomas was going to make a speech. And then she did her bit, going on, the Council this and the Council that since the year dot and everyone clapped and another chap thanked the Chairman of the County Council.' *Logical presentation of a century's achievements.* 'A racket broke out and I just stood. She'd never said. In all those years. Hadn't expected me to be interested. Too thick to understand.'

Sheila's head jerks sideways.

'It's true. Not sure I mind really. What really got me was what happened next—we were standing about clutching our teas shouting at each other and there was a series of loud raps. After a bit it all died down, and there was this same man standing behind the table with Mummy handing her this enormous knife. And she smiled and took it, pointed the tip so neatly, so carefully and slid it into the exact centre of that cake. A birthday cake. Sheila, think about it. A birthday cake. Made me think—something your mother said, years ago, 'a very unhappy woman'. But she looked happy gazing down on that cake. Don't know why I'm telling you all this. It's not important.' She lays down the spoon. 'What I saw then—she really thought baking a cake was beyond her. But then Aunt Peggy took to turning up with a birthday cake for me each year. I thought at the time—do when you're little, don't you?—she did it because she liked me.' She pauses, then resumes. 'Maybe, realistically, she wanted to annoy Mummy. The pair of them never got on. So you see, when I saw the way Mummy was looking at this cake which wasn't anything like as good as it could be, I thought maybe, really, secretly, she'd always wanted cakes, been too proud to admit she couldn't manage it. She is proud, isn't she?

Sheila seems to be counting the freckles on the back of the hand stretched across the table. Eventually she looks up. 'Well, you know your mother. You sure—about this afternoon?'

'Why not?'

'Your mother—'

'Can be awkward sometimes. Basically though—' her voice firms up, 'what I really don't understand—why she wanted to put herself in that place. Nothing wrong with it—very good in its way but we could've made things really nice for her here. The stables would make a wonderful granny-flat —John offered—'

'Joanne,' Sheila tries to distract her, 'her pony?'

'Always so late back. School runs a special bus out this way and we're pretty well the end of the route. Would've preferred to have her in Fairhurst. However—' Her head turns toward the window, turns back. 'An Exmoor can carry an adult, of course. But—and Daphne Manners offered to take him off her.'

'Hard on Jo.'

'Comes to us all—this growing up business.' Kate frowns, tapping the table. 'Can't always see logic the way Mummy does,' squares, triangles, circles, round and round, 'but this dumping herself in Gilbridge? '

Sheila goes on inspecting the back of her hand.

Kate's fingers bunch together, almost a fist. 'She can leave you feeling you've been cut into neat strips.' Her glance slides across Aga, dresser, blue and white crockery. 'But now, just sometimes, when you say something to her—'

Sheila's hand slides forward. 'Think I'll help myself to another of those biscuits. What did you say you called them? You know, Kate, your mother must have reasons. She always has.'

'Bachelor's buttons. Yes, well, I've never understood.'

'Be kind to yourself. She's old, you know and old people—you know.' Sheila glances at the clock. 'Sorry, must run.' She sweeps up her shopping bag. 'Sitting here won't butter any parsnips as Mum used to say.'

'I remember.' Kate's face briefly lights up but Sheila's half-way to the door. 'Got to be in Earlhampton by one'

'Meeting your friend. Yes.'

Sheila pauses with one hand on the door. 'Look, Kate, I'm sorry. This actually is almost the only purely social call I've made since I got back. Even this visit in Earlhampton's not pure friendship. Question about suppliers to sort out.' Her face softens, she smiles. 'Really must go.'

'Come again soon.'

'When the whirl dies down. You come to me next time.'

'Sure.'

She watches as a neat figure in grey trousers and a check seersucker blouse turns back into a shape in the doorway, then hair shining past the window. After that she collects the dirty mugs, washes them, hangs them slowly on their hooks on the green painted dresser. Mrs. Forster's was brown. The knots showed dully through the varnish. The room always warm.

The kitchen's turned grey, almost as if Old Flowery's still sitting in exactly that chair.

Morbid to stand here staring at shadows. Kate straightens her shoulders. Meant for some time to have a go at that cupboard. She swings open the door, takes down a pile of cups. Hmm, could do with a going over.

No sooner than Mummy was off out, Flowery'd dump herself on the chair, stretch out her legs, light a fag. Perm falling out, grimy overall. She runs warm water into the bowl, squirts in Fairy Liquid

A grin slides across her lips. *Boobs like saggy beachballs.* Mustn't let on you've heard. Beccy Elms last Thursday. Bit of a loudmouth. *'Come on, girls. Hang your coats on the hooks and wash your hands,'* listening—though shouldn't—who was she getting at? Hoping—? Surely not. That mouth gets Beccy into trouble. Roaming the streets till all hours. Next morning expected to measure out grams and tea-spoonfuls? *Me mum says I don't need any of this.* Probably don't in their house. But once she's got it off her chest no fool. Those *boobs?* Suited the person concerned only too well.

Old Flowery's even larger and more saggy. Did she really have only one overall? Several? All equally grubby?

Don't you go slipping off down to the station.

No, Mrs. Flowers.

That Brenda Forster. Slacking if you ask me. You don't want to be mixing with that type even if your—mummy—does let you go down there. Doesn't know, I reckon. Strutting about the place in men's clothes. Bren Gun, they call her. Why waste time thinking of her? A foul woman and Mummy away out in her green uniform.

The garden always there.

She raises her head gazing through the plum tree and wall behind it. Phil and Petronella had always been there, shadows under the pink horse chestnut. Run up and down the lawn in threes passing the ball, catching throws impossible at school, sneaking them some underarms you didn't let go of, much cleverer than ever managed elsewhere, but they'd always get them and let someone who never shot goals slam in several. Fantasy. Bad for the character? She shrugs, smiles. If Old Flowery had come nosing out she couldn't have said anything because she wouldn't have been able to see them.

What's the matter this morning to keep thinking of her?

Mrs Forster had no choice but to wear that thick blue uniform with trousers—scratchy. Got through a lot of Nivea. She tossed cases and boxes up into the guard's van as if they didn't weigh anything, barked out a list of stations, Fairhurst, Bagham, Illington Junction, Swailton Halt, Gilbridge—She peers into a cup. How'd that grey coating get there? Brindford, Fairspring, Cradlehurst, Marbleham. The voice rising to the end of the list, letting out its music, the same way you heard later at Bromley, the long line of names swooping up to *Herne Hill, Brixton and Victoria,* as if it would be a great triumph to get there.

She's getting through the cups now, slowly, gazing out of the window—Mrs Forster wasn't *barking,* just giving each name its length and weight as if chanting a psalm. And there's that path outside, hidden under the window, but every crack and smoothness so familiar, turn left outside the back door, right in the yard, down the drive into the lane, less than a mile downhill, running, careering round the corners and there was the station and now the house is fenced off from a decaying platform, its attention turned away from the space where the rails were towards that stringy lane to Spindlesham. Mrs Forster in 3 Main Road Terrace. All day in that chair.

Boxes, suitcases, bundles of newspapers, whatever, you name it—Mrs Forster heaved them just like the men. Four crates one after another. Trolley piled high and her wheeling it off, swinging them up to the guard with both arms. Watched with awe. And loved her. *What you two up to?* She stood where we squatted prodding at boxes of sort of soft yellowy-cream cardboard, DAY OLD CHICKS WITH CARE The chicks cheeping inside. Pair of us, supporting elbows on bare knees, peering in at the holes, trying to poke fingers though. Sheila's long and slender, really nice. Still beautiful. Had a good look.

She was afraid the chicks might miss their mothers. Her mother said no, hatched in an incubator and carried the boxes away from us to a shady corner.

That's the cups finished. She stacks them inside one another. Mrs. Forster all day in that chair, explaining, *No-one to bake for now.* As if that was all it was.

Do the rest another day. She jiggles them into the gap between her plates and Mummy's Wedgwood with roses.

For goodness sake, watch what you're doing—but always. always careful. Still even now can't help that tension—*not sensible to risk random damage.* Why not smash the whole lot into tiny pieces? Take it out into the garden and throw it on the stones? Cluttering the place. Not cluttering, no. Sell it? Can't sweep your mother out of the house. Intolerable. Some things had to go of course—*things have no value in themselves.* Don't they? John tough minded. *She says she's taken what she needs, get rid of the lot.* And he dealt with the auction house.

But not the corner cupboard, not her coffee cups, not the toasting fork. Only remember her using it once, but always the hope there's be another time; not the grey curtains in her bedroom, not this Wedgwood that was a wedding present. *No value in themselves?* Of course Mummy's not wrong; it's—that it's not always possible to feel exactly the way she does.

She eases the door shut. Cupboard tends to shake. One day —perhaps—when—not nice to think of when—when there could be another row of hanging cupboards above those shining tiles. Now in each of those already there there's a clot of darkness similar to that caused by the Wedgwood. She glances at the clock, then at the cake in its box, wipes her hand across her face. Put feet up? Be sitting all afternoon. With Mummy in that overcrowded room. So what then? New syllabus? Getting urgent but—

Vanilla cheesecake? Jo's birthday treat. She shall have it today. For coming to Parson's avenue? Shouldn't need a reward—but what an afternoon, not much fun for her.

Ought to be stricter? Sheila's father—lovely man, in spite of how he didn't look it—pale, scratchy moustache—caught us drawing a hopscotch on the platform. Better he said—swinging that leg, field glasses at the ready—learn how to tell Dorniers and Messerschmitts from Lancasters and Spitfires by their shape. Off-duty sling the glasses round his neck, limp off up to the look-out post; Observer Corps, hours alone watching on the hill. Make notes. Dash to nearest telephone. *Something coming in from somewhere heading towards somewhere else.*

He took away our chalk. Sheila laughed. Always good for a laugh. And where is Jo? No laugh when that young madam comes in.

But still, but still. Vanilla cheesecake. She reaches for Katie Stewart, *The Calendar Cookery Book*, slowly turns the pages. Mummy chewing her lips over a birthday treat. Not out that day in her uniform, doing whatever it was she did, thinking what it was she thought, but there in the dining-room, watching red fingernails on a white and silver box, soft hands lowering it onto the table, Aunt Peggy bending over it, then popping a look sideways. *Hope you don't mind, Alice, but I simply couldn't resist it.*

Wrinkled claws pulling up flaps. Huge green stone, half buried in chalky skin close to the knuckle, disappearing as the fingers slid inside and this smooth whiteness rose out of the box. Iced, with a ring of candles, each carried by a gnome riding a tortoise. From the other side of the table that clear pronouncement, *How splendid, Peggy—but really—it's too much. Wake up, Kate, say thank you.*

Grip the other box, the small one, whatever day that was, Aunt Peggy in the centre of the sitting-room, green hat cutting across the electric light, skirt flowing over her hips. Cut on the cross. Holding out her hand with that packet, six inches of it, that's all, soft dark blue paper. Tissue paper always white but that was dark blue. Day, must have been birthday, begun badly—Mummy cross, rain—her suddenly there. *Don't you want to see what's in it?*

Untie the string, coil it, place the coil on the table—tends to unroll, careful. Unfold paper, pull out a long white box, look, take off the lid and there—three pairs of hair-ribbons showing through tissue paper, pick them out one by one, violet, pale blue, scarlet.

Scarlet? For a gipsy—or wild Irish Kathleen—not plain Kate. Still in its box today, hiding at the back of a right-hand top drawer, still unworn.

And violet's not anything anyone can get hold of—half-way to mist. Yet today—eight violets spaced round the top of a white cake?

That day, rain streaming over the windows, the walls grey, you touched blue hair-ribbons, thought of clear sky. *Thank you, Aunt Peggy.* Met eyes sharp as a witch's gimlet. She bent away again waving the knife, cut two large slices. *I imagine you don't want one, Alice?* And when she'd gone taking the gnomes *for safety.*

Could I take it to Sheila's, Mummy? Afraid she'd throw it away? Thinking more how Mrs Forster'd get all excited and Sheila'd want a look and Mr.Forster'd come in and we'd all be crammed together in that warm kitchen? Waiting for an answer. At last a shrug. *If that's what you want.*

All the same, to be honest, not easy to like Aunt Peggy in spite of she was so kind—flabby cheeks caked with powder; teeth smeared with lipstick, eyes too green, hand waving one of those long cigarette holders in the affected way they did then, putting it to her mouth, blowing a smoke-ring, hooping it back out, leaning back in the arm-chair, stretching out one high-heeled foot, looking at Mummy.

Smoking's a dirty habit. Your aunt does it deliberately to provoke. Years later Daddy leaving packets of cigarettes lying about half-empty. Different of course. Just him.

She tracks down page 76, murmurs the list, butter, digestives, reaching each down in turn, cottage cheese—lucky there's an unopened carton, must be inspired this morning—eggs, castor, cornflour, vanilla—soured cream? Nope. Wasn't planning on this. Look at that clock. Mummy can't stand being kept waiting.

She stood waiting like a wired explosive. Three thirty-two late again. He was the only one got off. So wot? Where's this picture come from? Everything's churned together. She keeps her eyes off the folder lying on the dresser. *Food technology. Yuck,* as the girls say. *Cookery,* that's what it's all about. Feel heavy all over this morning. Thoughts all over the place.

Jo, when she was little, asked peculiar questions. *What is the sky made of? Why does Nutmeg have four feet and I've only two?* All you can do, smile, say don't know. Sometimes even now—way out, wild ideas. Need to bring her down to earth.

3

Half an hour she's stirring again, looking across the room at her books when a shy tap interrupts her solitude. A bell, very far off but one keeps hearing it. She strains towards it, but where? Something she has to hear that keeps coming. And a scent. There was a cloud of sickly smoke. A second soft tap isn't a bell and demands attention. Miss McDonald of course. Does the woman imagine the door's made of egg-shell? Lucky there's not a bus going past. She considers the possibility of not hearing; not that one resents the intrusion, though one has not issued an invitation—or has one?

She sighs. 'Come in,' and stares steadily as the other woman stands just over the threshold, a thin uncertain shape, botched together out of beige flannel, clasping a white envelope, bobbing up and down like a dipper, looking all round. No sense of authority there, and in Miss McDonald's position, one would have thought something of that sort was needed.

'Fire working?' She flits across the room and switches it on, 'Not, of course, that Pete needs supervising. Would you like to keep it on—if you've got visitors coming? Old house can be chilly, even in May. Pity—but there it is.'

Visitors. What's she mean, visitors? 'It's warm enough, thank you.'

'I've brought you your post.' She holds out a square white envelope. 'Birthday card, d'you think?' She bobs again, smiling, bright as a small bird summing up a pool in a river. 'Couldn't help wondering. Your nephew, you know, Bob, came to see you, didn't he, about six weeks ago, wasn't it? Fine young man, coming to visit his aunt. I remember his signature in the visitor's book, very firm handwriting—that's a real man's handwriting I thought and today this is it on the envelope, isn't it?'

Alice jerks upright. 'How did he know? Who told him?' Glaring as if she holds her accountable. Then she breathes in and speaks icily. 'Most kind of you to bring it.'

The housekeeper stands there holding the envelope. After a minute she remarks, 'I'll put it on the table beside you, shall I?' She goes on looking, her brow furrowed, seems to come to a decision. 'And your family coming. So nice to see them.'

'Who asked them to come?'

The eyes narrow but the voice softens. 'Perhaps they just want to?'

Alice stares, clasping the arms of the chair. She looks wildly round the room. 'Why should they come on Sunday?' That bell is still ringing and Kate—Kate is irrational.

'It's Saturday, Mrs. Lomas,' Miss McDonald says gently. 'You'll need an extra chair.' She studies the other woman's face. 'It's no problem. We can easily supply one.'

The woman's obsessed with that thing one sits on. Alice braces herself to deal with the question once and for all. 'One can find one's own way to the WC.'

Miss McDonald starts, frowns, a sparkle appears in her eyes and is suppressed. 'I think, Mrs. Lomas—only two comfortable chairs and this afternoon there'll be three of you.'

'One is sufficient. We don't need one each.'

Miss McDonald pauses again, the corners of her lips soften, she comes closer and touches the arm of her chair. 'This one you're sitting in and that over there.'

Alice regards them slowly, counting. 'Yes, that is two.'

'For three people an extra maybe?'

For a minute, Alice's shoulders tense. Then old formulae come wandering in. She raises her head. 'Thank you. Most kind, I'm sure.'

Miss McDonald's gaze steadies. 'These visits can be tiring.' then her face lights up again. 'I'm sure they won't stay long. Just your daughter and grand-daughter. Popping in to give you their greetings.' She turns away, then back, makes that little bob that isn't a curtsey, more a spring in the knees that can't be suppressed. 'Really, Mrs. Lomas, I'm sure it'll all turn out all right. Don't worry. We'll see you at lunchtime.'

Alice bows her head.

She goes on sitting after the door closes, hands still clasping the arms of the chair, feeling the comfort of elbows pressed in against her sides. At times nowadays the mouth opens, lips separating like branches in a hedge blown apart by the wind, words fly out. Gradually the room gathers round her, strong verticals, calm horizontals, calculable curves. One thanked that woman. Definitely one said, 'Thank you.' She leaves the envelope lying where it is.

She said she'd bring one of those objects. Where has she put it? Always need to keep an eye open. She pushes herself out of her chair, hobbles across to the corner by the door. Examines it carefully. Nothing there. That's good. She returns and subsides into her seat. That woman said, Bob. Why? Who's Bob? She shifts her right hip, stares at this strange white wall in front of her. There's a need to be sure.

White silk stockings and button strap shoes. On the lawn. Always on the lawn on Speech Days. Peggy with her hat slanted at an angle of roughly 60°, calling one Miss Hearn, with Natasha beside her—Peggy smiling in white silk stockings, *Barely average at maths is she, Miss Hearn?* She adjusts that point of hair beside her left ear, sliding her eyes toward to her brother, *I'm not sure I ever managed to reach average myself. Hopeless, wasn't I, George?* Pleased with herself. Impossible woman

Alice leans back, forehead, cheeks, mouth smooth out. Things are coming clear.

The sun always warm on Speech Day. George's shoes gleaming, him slim in a grey suit. Tinkle of tea-cups. The maids serving from those trestle tables the men set out beside the hall door. Tramp, tramp outside the classroom windows from 10.30 onwards. How one knows it's Speech Day—men outside the windows tramping round from the store-room beside the old stables, the girls turning to watch them, vaguer than ever, someone pulling a plait forward over her shoulder, fondling it with sideways looks. *Sorry, Miss Hearn, I thought you meant the angle at the top, that kind of slopey one.*

After the speeches one stands in the garden and makes the necessary effort to talk to women no more sensible than their daughters, wasting one's life.

She's never seen this room before. Where? Where? What is one doing here? Where is the sense in the world? She fixes each piece of furniture with desperation. That's Father's bureau. How did it get here? That's one's bed. Does one sleep here? Why not at home? Then, very distantly, that bell rings again and those are one's own bookshelves. Framed by a white wall. This shining clarity seems familiar, how things should be, though not quite. This isn't Holmbush. One can be clear on that. But one's effects are here, it seems probable one chose to have them here. It's all in the will. One is invariably correct when one follows reason. And this envelope here on the table, containing, apparently, a card from 'Bob'?

That's that then. Her head drops forward but she's not asleep. She's sure of that. *Hallo, George, look, it's spittering with rain.*

Pity—he pulls up the hood of the Oxford and snaps it into position, *you won't see much but I can't have you getting wet.*

As soon as he's on the road he's showing off. A very smooth ride. Oh yes, George, you know how to drive—and you know quality, not just in a car to do you justice.

Circle your hand, oh so neatly, turning right. That's you, incapable of a sloppy gesture, loading your rifle, fastening pop-studs, dancing, measuring medicine—every movement of yours has that exactitude. All there is to you. One is taken in.

You're turning left now off the tar onto the centre of a wide cart track. You know somewhere one's *bound to love.*

On either side, a hedge, loaded with haws. Not far ahead, a stand of beech, the sun shining again as if clouds never happen.

You draw into the shade, pull up, leap out. *Wait now.* You reach into the back of the car, heave out a wicker basket and a dark blue travelling rug.

One can't sit in the passenger seat for ever staring like a wooden doll. And there's that envelope again. How did it get here? Did one ask for it? No need to touch it.

Bob, she said. The freckles that go with red hair. Large feet. Not George's boy. Not Peggy's. He's sent a card. And then it comes like a burst of sunlight—Natasha's son. Red hair runs in that family.

11.25 a.m.

When she reaches the glade the trees have become friendlier. She leans her hand on the nearest trunk. Smooth, warm, a beech. Plenty of time to look at the wood.

Caw of a distant crow. Something, most probably a pheasant, screeches beyond the brambles. She waits. No tree-creeper flies down to start its scuttle up and round from the base of a trunk, no blackbird tosses dead leaves, no squirrel curls its tail over its back, observing. No need to get in yet. Why go in at all? Whole world—out there. Where? How?

She stares at the roots of the beech trees, the way they snake across the ground, the grey bark that somehow manages to be almost shiny and looks as if it's not properly fastened on, as if it could slide across what's underneath, muscles, flesh, whatever, like the crumpled hide of a hippo; but these creatures would be snakes—no, bigger than snakes—serpents; they seem to have writhed and then become fixed, half out of the earth. Which makes them really evil. She goes on staring. Really, really evil if you look at them like that. Do for *Star Wars*. Monsters trying to trap Darth Vader.

Star Wars brill? Some of them think so. Myself, not sold on space. Nor Shaz neither. We always think the same. Till now. Brill, isn't it? Totally, utterly brill.

Gaga, completely gaga. Dad, a voice through the door. Me in the hall listening, Gran sort of hanging about at the back of my mind. Which was obviously completely off-point.

You've always said she's a very capable woman.

Face facts, Kate. She's gaga, off with the fairies.

She understood enough to keep her brother from laying hands on the house. Definitely not Gran. *You said so. Good head on her, you said*—Mum in don't-tell-me-stories mode.

For heaven's sake stop shilly-shallying.

Mum does but he didn't need to say so, so I barged in and he barked, *What you think you're you doing down here?*

Had every right. *Don't talk to Mum like that.* Or to me either.

His mouth opened and Mum came in all flustered. *He's quite right, Jo,* apologising.

Who's gaga?

Mind your own business/Don't use that word. Pair of them together.

Dad just did.

Great inbreath. Mum lays her hand on his arm. *What about your homework, Jo?*

Done it, and Dad had to bring up Gran was paying good money for St. Anne's.

Didn't ask her to, did I?

Jo, Mum behind him, coming forward, *Jo. Please.*

Slacking. Totally not fair. Can't help it if I work fast. *Have finished. All easy stuff.* Why can't they believe me? Biology, English, French. Most of them a doddle. Nothing wrong with my marks if they care to look.

John, Mum in front of him now.

He backed down, huffing a bit, then, *If you've got all that time to spare you might consider giving a hand with the grass.*

So who? Question kept nagging. Mum said, *No-one you know. Something that happens to some people when they get older. Very sad.* Keeping her eyes headed down onto the saucepan, taking care not to push her hair back off her face. Which was a bit flushed. *Not to everybody, Jo.* Kind of muttered. *Just some people.* Something in her voice, very deep, trying to be sincere, like when explaining The Facts. *Mostly it doesn't happen, Jo. Only to some people.*

Which ones?

Head down, stirring. *People who haven't kept their brains active enough, probably.*

But—

She let go of the spoon and grabbed the handle. *There, that's that. Be a lamb, pass me that bowl.*

The *lamb* reached out.

But Gran went on and on. *Which day of the week is it? Tuesday?* We kept telling her it was Wednesday.

Obviously couldn't be Gran they meant. That a stupid idea from the first. There was that old lady of course, old witch, old hag. Who wants to go to Andover. But Dad wouldn't know her. Shouldn't really call her a hag—but—way she looks and her hair. People shouldn't let themselves get like that, gaga, off their rocker. Can't help it? *Something that happens?* Maybe they can't help it but it's all wrong. The world's all wrong? Feels like that and nothing you can do. Why did Gran want to put herself in that place?

Better than letting her have the stable? That would've been a total, absolute disaster.

Brill to have small place of your own. When you've been in a house most of your life but the main part's too big? Back Lane was smaller, but ace.

Gran never used to shout. Face always an ice-block, all sharp angles—stalagmite or—tite? Shouted, really, genuinely shouted. Mum always agitates, that's the trouble. Gran knew what she wanted.

She drops her hand from the tree, still stands. Wouldn't be so bad having to go to that place if I thought it would do any good.

11.37 a.m.

Why remember Mrs Forster was on duty that day when the 3.32 came in? Seems no point, but feel her solid, there in the background. Remember foot rubbing against back of leg, up and down, sole of shoe on bare skin, Mummy standing stiff. *Do stop fidgeting, Kate.* The train slowing, stopping. The blank wall of the sides of three carriages. Only one door swung open, thin man in a grey overcoat climbed down. *For heaven's sake*—Mummy's finger a skewer driven in—*run to your father.* She stayed where she was.

Close up, grasped by this man, who smelt of cigarettes? How could anyone have such tight arms? Mustn't wriggle against them. *He's your father.* Only three when he went away. He'd become like someone in a story. *Your father's a very intelligent man. It's why he's away. Doing a very special job.*

She'd walked down. No, came in the car. Because of the suitcase. But for a child going ahead on foot dawdling, a lovely warm day, swallows lining the wires, spindleberries leaning across the trunk of the elm. Orange beads inside tiny pink cheeks. Knew them—though shouldn't have. However did *The Flower Fairies* penetrate our house? Fairy stories *not worth bothering with.* Lent by Mrs. Forster? In bed in the early morning, gazing at the Spindle-tree Fairy's clothes, tracing how they were shaped like petals, sepals and berries.

She picks up the folder, stares over it at her blue and white cups hanging on the dresser. He put his suitcase in the boot, moved towards the driver's door. She was there first, *If you don't mind, George.*

He flourished the door open. Later, watching her swing the car into the drive, *I shall need it to get into Gilbridge tomorrow.*

You can go on the train. The petrol ration is allocated to my work with the WVS.

All yours, madam.

But Mrs. Forster laughed, no matter what anyone said. *'Bren Gun' they call me in the village 'cos of the way I shout the names of the stations. Not much point if no-one can hear.* Another time, *I know what they say, She wears the trousers.* Huge chuckle. *Alfie'd never stand for me telling him what to do.* She rested the basket of wet sheets, propping her arms on the table. *Very lucky I was to get him.* Whenever he came in she'd smile. Happy ever after? Can be done, apparently. With John of course.

And today Sheila stood in the doorway, making the place feel different. Kate gazes round her kitchen, the room at Holmbush Daddy had hardly ever been into. Not a man's place. Whisked off, 1939, to this hush-hush place in the north. To design clever bullets. *A very intelligent man.* Mummy not sounding pleased.

She lays down the folder and drifts towards the cake. Only Aunt Peggy. Kind, very kind, but so different from us and Mummy used to look bullets. She stands gazing at the box. Wouldn't ever have risked it—but after what happened at County Hall—and violets so she can't turn her nose up at roses. Not as easy as roses.

Daddy took the train every day to Gilbridge. Never showed he minded. Never showed anything much; never talked about Uncle Fred or Uncle Arthur or Uncle Bill. Though every November, a poppy. *Your father has to believe it was worthwhile. He's very conventional.* Difficult for him. He'd no choice. Oldest so had to stay to look after the firm. Munitions. Essential war-work.

Mr Forster set on being ordinary. *None of your fancy ideas in this house,* stroking his moustache, *just good. sound, solid common sense.* Sheila shook him, passing the 11+. He and her mother chewed it over and over. *No-one in our family—What would your parents say, Kate?*

Mumbling, *Not sure, Mr. Forster;* then Sheila's face. *They'd probably think it was a good idea.* But pulling away—Mummy, convinced you'd fail, not even letting you try and she's now saying *Tuesday* when it's Saturday. Refusing to believe she's wrong. Obstinate, like all old people. But *Accuracy is of the essence?* Oh well.

She picks up the folder and carries it to the table, doesn't open it, leans her arms on the table, swinging her legs from that level bough of the Forster's Newton Wonder, singing to the birds with Sheila, laughing at what she said happened at her school, seeing steam getting nearer, running down to the platform as the doors opened. Counting how many get on or off. *Good afternoon, Mr. Tompkins, Mr Sanderling. Afternoon Sheila, helping your mother as usual?*

And there for me, the apple tree—the Newton Wonder that produced loads of apples.

In the autumn standing at Mrs. Forster's table coring them, measuring out flour and marge; rubbing the together the marge softening, merging with the flour, crumbs forming. Mrs Forster close behind, *Light hand you want with pastry.* All day now in that armchair, hardly denting the cushion but then *Lift your hands—like this. See how the bits drop back into the bowl? That way air gets in.* Then with her still watching, fold the dough round the fruit, slide a tray into the oven, later wrap a thick cloth over hands, lift out dumplings with firm crusts and a scent they hadn't had before.

The fragrance of dog rose, stitchwort, campion. Walking up home with Daddy, off the 6.03 that always had its engine on backwards. Pulled the carriages facing backwards Gilbridge to paper mill. Returned facing forwards, pushing. Never in the normal relationship. Worked. So what is normal, sensible, logical? Logic, logic, what's logic got to do with anything? *Oh god, Alice, do try to be human.* Aunt Peggy raising her eyes to the ceiling, sweeping her forehead with the back of her hand.

Mustn't take her side.

Let you go and sit there and take part in that superstition? All it was, Sheila'd joined the Church choir. Thought it would be nice go and hear her. *No child of mine.* No use begging. Face stiff as a carcass the butcher reaches down, lays on the board, gives a neat flick of the wrist, brings the cleaver down. Chop. *That's what wrecked your grandfather's life.* But Granddad, crouching at the bottom of the garden—*Some people might think this is cheating,* showing how to turn a conker into *a dead cert winner* by hardening it in the bonfire? He had this little smile.

And Sheila laughing, twirling round on one foot, waving her arms, coming back to stand serious. *Don't have to listen to it all, nice place to sit and think.* Older, standing still, she said,

It's the roof, I love the way the music goes up into the roof. You feel small but part of it. Liking to feel small. Which seemed odd then.

Feel better grappling with that syllabus?

Used to try to read the back page of *The Times* Daddy read on the train. Sitting opposite, prim maybe? School hat, grey gabardine; sat beside him when he got the Ford, watched the trees go past. And at four-o-clock down Limes Road, into Stambury Avenue, there at the end, our shop on the opposite side of the road, centre of the High Street, display of rods shining in the window. The bell rang, the door swung heavy. He peered out of the back room and smiled. *Come in here, Kate, and settle down to your homework. Not long till closing.*

She glances again at the clock. Moved on quite bit and still no sign. Mummy sitting in that room. Still no Jo. Time flying.

Can tie a fly He was very patient. In the shop one Saturday afternoon.

Told him in the little room at the back. A table in the centre, two stools. You had one, got him to sit at the other. The silence seemed endless—*Daddy*—risked it, pulled out the envelope out and he signed. A great big flourishing signature.

She drums her fingers on the table-top. Ought to get down to that syllabus. Not today, not now, somehow. So? Not that the cupboard's really bad. Just a matter of taking everything out, giving a quick wipe, replacing the old lining paper. putting it all back after a good read of the labels. Extraordinary how things lurk at the back for years

A few minutes later last year's jams are ranged across the table, gooseberry right, raspberry, strawberry, black currant centre, plum left, glass shining over dark shapes, transparent paper tops sparkling and behind them white tiles, some decorated with life-like tomatoes and cucumbers, white cupboard fronts with sliding doors. What a kitchen should look like.

At the institute they looked out on the garden, grass, an old-fashioned rose, grimy yellow brick walls. To reach them you went outside and along a tarmac path through the strange quiet of London. All those miles and miles of houses, all that traffic and yet you'd walk across a back garden and hear nothing. She fetches a cloth from the sink, begins wiping non-existent dust from shining jars.

Peeling gold letters on a brown board, *The Manners-Welbeck Institute of Domestic Arts, founded 1893.* Miles of grey pavement. Heaved up by the roots of plane trees. Their bobbles against the sky. Pay off the taxi-driver. Tip him. Daddy said 10%. Hand shaking,

And now she leans back and looks at this kitchen which was her mother's and is now on its way to growing to be hers, though sort of stuck half way, as it has to be while Mummy's alive even if she's not here—always this string running between Gilbridge and here as if she must be thinking about it, remembering, even if only how much she disliked it.

Why on earth did she get the jars out? Heavens above, look at the clock. What a mess and no time now to put them back. She pushes them into dead straight lines, heaves herself back onto her feet, gets out a loaf, marg, cheese, a knife. Sandwiches for her and Jo. A quick lunch. Blow! Just look at that. Jo's been at the apples. Don't buy them for that pony to devour. She wipes her hand across her face, applies the knife to the loaf.

11.45 a.m.

After another meandering trek the lav reveals itself, as one would of course expect, though lurking. Miss McDonald trying to insinuate one of those objects that stand in the room. Anyone with eyes can see them. No need to obtrude one's problems on other people, although, admittedly, one enjoys greater privacy here than at Holmbush—Kate never satisfied, wants to know everything—

And here's the door opening, Miss McDonald again, babbling on like a brook and with all its intelligence. 'A real pleasure to come into this room and still, after the months you've been here, the brightness so wonderfully unexpected. The committee were doubtful—well, it's not what we normally do for a new resident but as I said to them—the chairman of the County Council—'

County Council? What—?

'and the family are promising to restore it though perhaps that might not be needed—this white is so restful—someone else—you never know—and with furniture of the right period, which is exactly what you've brought. And the sun comes in here most of the day, so lovely and warm and bright.'

The traffic growls incessantly, the heat beats through closed windows. At Holmbush they stood open all summer and the breeze ran through the house.

One knows the sun. 'Oh the sun—the sun has too many worshippers.' She throws back her shoulders. 'One should have more respect for one's health.'

'Still, I hope you're comfortable here.' Miss McDonald considers the way Alice's chair has found its way into a shaft of sunlight. She smiles to herself and relaxes, as if she intends to give time to her visit. 'I do so love the scent of the limes and their branches are so beautiful to look out on. Makes me think how lucky we are.' Somewhere not far off there's a dull clatter like metal falling. A shadow crosses her face. 'Noisy work on a Saturday morning, so unnecessary, some of the residents will be upset, so unreasonable causing all this disturbance.' She crosses to the widow, glances up and down the street. 'Mrs Hebden says—she has a cousin in the building trade—who has a daughter in Easedale Street—just round the corner from here where all the building's going on and the daughter says they're delivering the stuff Saturdays so as not to waste money—though as she says since they've got to pay overtime, what are they really saving?' She turns back, comes closer, her face wrinkling. 'I do hope it's not disturbing you.'

Alice eyes her glassily and she breaks off—'Oh I do talk, don't I?'—swings back towards the door, goes out, returns dangling something brown—one of those objects? But no, legs too long. A freshly shot muntjac deer at the end of her arm. Stiff legs sprawling, hard little hooves rattling on the kitchen table. His voice, *Ever seen anything like this? Thought it was a rabbit hiding in the bracken. Got it first shot.* He would.

The room's full of bracken. Through a gap she sees Miss McDonald's eyes.

'He shot it. Came in grinning.' The gap's wider now and Miss McDonald is frowning through it as she announces, 'That's the chair you asked for, Mrs. Lomas. I'll put it over there by the table.'

A chair? Has one asked for a chair? No, one definitely has not. One wouldn't forget making a request of that sort. But —could one have thought of it? Could thinking produce a chair? She shifts her gaze from the housekeeper's uncomfortable eyes, peers at bookshelves, walls, table, braces herself against them. Is the woman up to her tricks again? 'I'm so sorry to put you to all this trouble—but—after all—my grand-daughter's not very likely to need that kind of thing.' She raises her head. 'I think, if you don't mind, it would be better to take it away. If she really needs it, though one can't imagine she would, I'll send her to ask for it. She'll know where to find you.'

'That's quite all right, Mrs. Lomas. There's absolutely no problem.' She increases the space between them and smiles gently. 'You're new to the house. Things can be very disconcerting.' And as Alice stiffens, 'I thought I'd better warn you—it's just what we do—very friendly but you haven't been here long and somehow birthdays get bunched —yours this week, Mrs Carton's next Monday, Mrs Brown next Thursday but in all the time since you arrived there's only been Mrs Waterson—'

Mrs Waterson? Who's Mrs Waterson?

'—and that must be nearly three months ago. You'd only just arrived so you might not remember. They'll give you a card, someone'll say a few words—I've no idea who—they don't tell me that sort of thing—we'll all sing 'Happy Birthday'. That's all. Nothing much.'

Explaining gently, as if one couldn't understand. As the dentist said, *Nothing much. Open wide* and in came that drill.

Alice firms up her face. 'Thank you for telling me, Miss McDonald. It's very kind of you to worry about me. Of course—' and at last the elusive formula emerges from a cloud, 'I shall be delighted—'

The housekeeper smiles again, clasping her hands. 'Must be on my way. Looking forward to lunchtime.'

'It's a table.'

Miss McDonald becomes completely still.

'A table.' There definitely was a table. With shaky legs.

'I'm sorry?'

'A table.' Surely the woman knows what a table is.

'I'm sorry, Mrs. Lomas—' Her voice is soft, threatening concern. One's slipped. Everything's slipped. 'I thought—' Pale face. So far away.

Alice breathes slowly in and straightens it all against the walls 'No matter.' And this is true. Whatever it was one had perceived has sunk away back into a void from which it emerged. 'We can forget it.' She sits up firmly and as she does so another formula arrives. 'Please don't worry. Thank you for your kindness.'

In the still after the door closes Alice sinks back into her chair. When someone insists on chattering it's an effort to hold onto the moment but it's rising again, an echo that can't be doubted—legs that rattled and fell all ways in a dark corridor that smelt of damp. A slatted door. A table. A number of tables, all the same. *I'm sure you're remembering the paint, aren't you Alice?* One extracted them from the back of the cupboard with a tilt intended to counteract the spiteful swing of the legs and every single time one was heaving one along the passage and up the stairs, *Remembering the paint, aren't you Alice?*

She's held by the clarity of those tables and Mother's voice making it all more difficult. A narrow passage half blocked by potted plants and whatnots carrying rose-bowls. Yes, in looking back one feels one has the right to object. One would never have tolerated storage arrangements like that at Holmbush. Why Mother saw fit to keep a tea-chest of unpacked crockery in front of the tables was a mystery. Perhaps because she never had to move it herself—and all that mess, clotheshorse, three tin trays, five kilner jars, a partridge in a pear tree—What partridge? Why? It seems to have pushed itself in where it's not wanted. She shakes her head. The room's so stuffy. Makes one sleepy. The legs swung as if aiming at one's ankles, and then, as one struggled to stand it and steady it, a broken strut bit one's fingers. Bad-tempered brutes, sealyhams among tables.

One pushed back armchairs and sofa. Forced the strut under the clip. Set the completed table in place. Three more to make a square.

For goodness sake, Alice. They're not on parade. Is that what they teach you at Girton? All those clever woman and they can't show you how to make a room look comfortable?

Is there anything else you'd like, Mother? A well brought up girl always asks that kind of question. *Anything else you'd like?*

Put out the scoring pads tidily, Alice. They look so much better placed across the corners of the table. People notice, you know. And a bowl of fresh roses on each of the side-tables.

A pair of hands laying packs of cards central, pads on precise diagonals. Light from the bay-window crossing at right-angles. Victorian. Not a Georgian area of Bath. A place that stays still while she contemplates a high room with mouldings and a well-shaped bay window and sees sunlight pouring over a small table tucked into a dormer—drain-pipes and chimneys, sparrows and starlings—clouds sometimes block the sunlight, now let it through, books and papers dazzle and dance. All is peace, peace and reason. Up here on the third floor, quiet, at the back one plunges into dimensions. How to imagine five? Six? How to handle them? One uses one's head then, pen and paper.

She leans back in her chair, closes her eyes. Watches things running the way they should. The beauty and the power of mathematics, of the logic, the austere, orderly progress of the mind from one point to another until the conclusion's inevitable and one sees its power. She nods. For the moment everything's clear and coherent at that small, rectangular table with a view slanting upwards towards the sky. Depths open and one sees how it has been possible for these seemingly abstruse theorems to allow a mathematician to discover a planet a century earlier than any astronomer. Learning to fly must be like this. One will never now be first, but one can still know the joy of handling a tool others have perfected. One closes one's eyes calling up the fifth dimension.

When she wakes the sun has moved off her legs. Voices float upwards through the house.

Two no trumps, really, partner…

Lloyd George...

You know what they say about him.

You should have passed.

Reparations—

To the last farthing.

One slides between them handing out plates and the conversation rattles past like a shower of bullets.

Make them pay.

Teach them what suffering really is.

My dear, her finger nails—

No sugar, thank you.

Make the brutes pay.

I'll have the egg and cress, if you don't mind.

A fixed smile walks through a no man's land where Father wanders at ease, listening, nodding, laughing at their jokes. How can he bring himself to be dragged from his study to waste time on dreary people and, after they've taken themselves off, on Mother's complaints?

Occasionally he went out. Parish business. That's how it was. It was....was....how....

She wakes again to uninvited words running in her head,

Thou hast conquered, O pale Galilean,

She examines them carefully.

The world has grown pale from thy breath.

O pale Galilean—They appear to want to repeat themselves over and over. *The world has grown pale...* Round and round. But one has never bought poetry.

They're mixed into the sound of metal, apparently through the limes—but not—a spoon grating on a cup. A young woman is stirring slowly, V—v—v—Violet that was it—smiling down at swirling cocoa. Then looking up. One couldn't escape her eyes, *Admit it, Alice, the Church has always been the enemy of reason.*

One took a job at St. Margaret's. This room is too big for St. Margaret's and no wash-stand. She looks all round, feels cold. How will one wash? Her breathing speeds up.

Her hands close tightly on the arms of her chair. Follow an arithmetical sequence. That is one's bed, that the sitting-room table one's known for years, that's Father's bureau. At St. Margaret's? What are they doing there? Can't be there. So where? Those are one's books. *Surely you don't need to take all of them, Mummy?* Kate, bleating. Shelves with the sun on them. *The brightness so wonderful.* Babble, babble, that brook. Ah, Gilbridge. Yes. One chose to live here. Entirely reasonable. What else could one do?

The sound of a bell. Again. Not a light trill this time but a relentless calling. Ring of trees, a pond. To the left of the church gate. The mist shaken by an early morning bell. Not the mathematical tracery of change-ringing. Ding, ding, in clammy half-dark. Advent, a season that indulges the

Church's most treasured threats, death, judgement, heaven, hell. The bell keeps repeating. Parallel lines never converge.

Wouldn't it better, Father, to have your own parish, not to be always taking services for other people? Mush of dead leaves clinging to one's shoes. One kept shaking them off.

There's a work to be done here, pressing forward obstinately into the mist, then slowed and turned, massive as Goliath, droplets of mist sparkling on that black coat. *You mustn't blame your mother.*

Of course not, Father.

She needs the life and the company here. Such a long look, reproachful, almost accusing. *My work can be done anywhere. There are always people who need a priest.*

Always....a priest—...need a—...priest—.... Shreds vanish into mist. She gazes vaguely at her hands. There they are lying in her lap. A minute later she raises her head.

You see, Alice, parallel lines never meet. There they are running off, circling the globe, side by side out into space. *Really never, father? Never ever?* One sits on the floor at his feet, looking up.

Look at the state of your fingers. No, don't wipe them on your pinny. Here's a piece of paper.

The fire flickering in the grate, in front of them, the hearth. One's finger traces lines on the tiles, thin yellow on dark green, in and out of each other, triangles interlocking with squares, octagons, weaving in and out, discerning a pattern. One sits at his feet finding the sense in it. Following reason.

These ones aren't parallel.

He smiles, *They meet and cross, an intricate pattern. Don't you think that's interesting?*

He has books on his shelves in German, Greek and Hebrew. The bishop wants him to write.

But now parallel lines are converging. *You mustn't blame your mother.*

One follows him—hurrying now—scuffing one's feet through the compost, through the porch into gloom and darkness. In daylight one has a clear view of etiolated saints in robes of vitriolic blue and green cramped inside Victorian Gothic windows. At 8.00 on a December morning the leads weave outlines of shining black, the glass is charcoal. One expects that, of course. One's seen it all before. *You mustn't blame your mother.*

Lumpy overcoats, in twos and threes at intervals over the church, arms propped on the back of pew in front, heads resting on them, men distinguished by white hair or shining baldness. Under their hats the women may be dummies. All sunk, in prayer, presumably.

One's heels clatter on tiles, one slides into in a back pew, starts to kneel but can't. It's impossible, the choking hypocrisy of it—just to please Father. She's hit full in the chest. Strange how sudden. Until precisely that morning one's seen no harm.

One's rigid and amazed. The congregation heave themselves to their feet, an alb swishes past, Father attains the chancel steps. *Our Father...* No need to grit one's teeth at those well-worn words as they flow pitilessly on and on, knees feeling a pull downward—it's here now, pulling her down, so well built in. Her hands find the chair arms. She pushes herself up, wanders towards the window. That's where the light's coming from—filtering through the leaves of the lime-trees—candle-light shifting. How interesting it is. Thin smoke rises to touch the dark-faced saints with wisps of charity. From how many altars? How many faiths? That same grey smoke?

The censer rattles, a cloud of sickly smoke. Father faces the altar, raises the cup to the full length of his arms. White sleeves fall back. He pronounces each word of consecration distinctly, almost pedantically, drained of emotion.

She stares down into Parson's Avenue. The confusion of those tree-tops. The frown deepens between her eye-brows. Somewhere there's tension. The church seems full of it. Where is it? It can't be among the congregation. They appear to be asleep.

He turns again towards the nave and holds out this *mystery*. It rests in his hands, a gracious nestling he's going to put into the hands of the people. *Take, eat.* Take in his face, the trained lack of expression—the shock of it—so different from normal. That's what it is to be a priest—yes, that's what is—hidden under those leaves. They're stirring now, a little wind. So much power. He believes he has so much power.

Priests and wizards, seers and soothsayers, one can go on, find title after title, pre-historic, prehistoric tribe, imagining they can release *The Power*. Why are the leaves shaking? It's not reasonable for them to shake. Nothing is reasonable. Standing here feeling one's arms tremble, thinking about things that aren't reasonable. Leaves shaking together. One can't walk on shaking leaves. For a moment she stands dazed, then reaches out to an upright window-bar, grips it, goes on waiting. At last she takes a deep breath and turns back into the room. One can control one's mind.

It has to be admitted, Father was not reasonable. An intelligent, twentieth-century man, the ex-rector of Ferdington, unfortunately retired to Bath—which could have helped him—he was surrounded by monuments of the most rational period of all English history. Smooth shaven—though dog-collared—should have had nothing in common with a witch-doctor prancing in a fury of feather dusters. But he had. One knew then, for certain.

He was moving deliberately down the line of worshippers. *This is my body.* He displayed the wafer, lowered it precisely into hands cupped to receive it. He was absorbed, walking, he imagined, on the edge between two realities.

Then reality struck home. One perceived how he had fallen victim to the Christ who enticed him through the sweet power of the Mass. *Sacrifice yourself, lay down your interests, your talent, crucify your own personality, and in return you shall have the power of the greatest mystery. You shall hold in your own hands the aweful bread and wine.* In everyday life, he was Mother's doormat. That didn't matter to him. In fact what could better fit his dream? The greater his humiliation, the greater his glory.

One sat alone in the back pew observing, while dark figures waddled back to their seats. What a procession of smug faces.

In spite of himself, Father did one good thing that morning. He demonstrated what happens if one allows oneself to be guided by anything other than reason. In that moment it became clear the only way to live is to follow reason. One must never deviate as he deviated. At 8.30 on the second Sunday in Advent, in the year of one's twenty-first birthday, Father taught a useful lesson.

She settles back in her chair. Everything is in place now. It is good to remember so clearly. She shuts her eyes. We can go home now. Fog is lifting, a lemon sun fingering bare branches.

12.02 p.m.

Lettuces are standing up nicely, doing well this year. She squats down, begins to break off leaves one by one, 'Cut-and-Come-Again', new variety; worth having. The sun's warm on her back and when she stands up only a few minutes have gone.

She gathers in a scent, faint here among the vegetables but nice, seeping through from somewhere else. Wisteria, of course, outside old bedroom window. Small kid last thing, just getting dark, nose and cheeks down into those cool petals. *Kate wallowing in scent.* Footsteps on the stairs, shoulders jerked inside and the sweetness fading. Now on the garden path, carrying a handful of lettuce towards the top terrace, silk on the air.

And immediately to the right now may blossom, rich like ice cream—learned the hard way not to put face in too deep. She turns towards it all the same. Something harsh and strange has somehow mixed itself in with it today, this other scent, that's suddenly come back and is hanging about, like the peculiar taste of a metal spoon when eating a boiled egg. At the same time sweet.

Dark, slowly becoming lighter. Most people would've said it was cold. And this thin scent with an edge to it—very odd—made the place feel warm. Came in to get out of the rain. Pounding down outside, couldn't hear it in here. Grey day but could make out colours in the windows, strong blue, rich red, off-key green, robes, the angels' white wings. Even without light shining through. Other days when sun came out, red, green, blue jellyfish floating over the pews. See-through like angels. If they exist their bodies have to be invisible clouds, wisteria scent.

And the whole place lifting. Sheila loved the way the singing rose into the roof at St. Mary's, which isn't that high. All Saints' beams much higher, blacker. Comfortable in both to be small. Not despicable, simply right. That's how it is. Good to be small, ordinary.

She rests her arms on the terrace wall. The sun today's at its best. She feels solid, looking down over the valley to those woods—umbrella shapes of pines on the rise to the left, lower down the dome of the oak where the rooks nest, in front of them all, the birches at the back end of Anglands field. No invisible line pulls her towards Fairhurst. The warm stone grounds her. Have come here lots of times—Mummy's said something—elbows on this, begin to feel real.

No pheasants today. Always in late summer, lean arms on stone, watch them jabbing across the lawn, one step at a time little sideways darts. Daddy didn't know what they were taking—seeds? Tiny insects? Side by side watching glorious birds.

*

Way up from the station Daddy sometimes turned off into Blacklers Woods. Path like walking on a quilt, scattered with green, spiky husks, brown, not as rich as conkers but just as shiny, peeping through cracks. Grab up sweet chestnuts—first one for him—his thumb and first fingertip gripping the skin, peeling it off in strips, him half smiling as he chewed; twelve year old in heavy shoes looking up, eating one too. Her smile deepens. Raw, chalky, the pith a little bitter. Ate them between lessons. Also under the desk, nails getting jammed up with shreds of skin, waiting till whoever it was turned to the blackboard, popping in the nut, chewing in the smell of chalk, caked ink and dingy wood, trees coming back and the sound of a wood pigeon. She smiles and leans forward. Trout in the pool below the waterfall. Don't see them at first, then do, quivering shadows. facing upstream, water rushing through their gills.

Daddy said an angler'd drop a fly light as anything, bang under a fish's nose. *How'd he know where the nose is, Daddy? There's a little hump in the water. Can he really see it? When he's learnt what to watch for. Can you see it? Not an angler.* He liked shooting, but, *Need to understand what customers want.*

How to tie a Grey Wullf. *An old fly now but always good for a chalk stream.* Wet Saturday in March, no-one coming into the shop, table in back room moved so that light came from the side. The hook held in the clamp, his fingers twisting round the shaft, *If you put too much weight on the thread it breaks.* Attaching the bucktail for the wing, fanning it out, fastening on fragments of feather to shape a downy body and the whole thing so light, so clever and an angler could tell from the state of the water exactly where to cast so it landed under the nose of a trout that'd be fooled into thinking it was a mayfly

Mummy—logical to eat other creatures—order of nature—Logic, logic—and a week ago she insisted it was Thursday when it was Saturday, didn't look properly at diary held under her nose though always, always in the past, had always been so keen on getting things right—and facts, *hard facts. Face up to facts.* The way she looked at Daddy—*One prefers not to kill for fun.*

Keep everything nice this afternoon. She firms her elbows down onto the hard surface. Out here with all this air and the view down onto trees has always been a place to think of nice things.

Like in the shop, in the little room at the back, behind the door unlocked at the end of the day when he'd put money in the safe and check the guns. Shelves piled with stock. Reels, flies. hooks, one small window above the cupboards. Glass shining dark, shot-guns, little gleams among blurs, cartridges. Small-bore in another room he was the only one ever went into.

Always a ditherer, standing in the place where customers would often stop to look round before they made up their minds, at last slipping the stool out from behind the counter, taking it through, plonking it down at that dark wooden table with the sticky drawer, the one where Roger found the letters. Clearing out Daddy's things. *Some of this seems to be personal. Would you like to take them, Kate?* Nice man. Funny little dimple in his right cheek. Glad he's got the business.

Took them up to the bedroom, sat on the bed feeling the bundle. He'd kept them all. She creases her eyes, hears words running through the mind of a girl who's forming each sentence before she writes.

Dear Daddy,

thank you for taking me to the station. I had a good journey and got a taxi quite easily at Waterloo. The man was very nice and dropped me right outside. I have a nice room on the second floor, sharing with a girl from Newcastle called Marion. You were up that way in the war, weren't you? She's a bit scatty but very nice really.

Grown woman sitting on a double bed, reading this ancient stuff, feeling she's spying.

There are forty of us in my year. They all look nice and friendly though some of them talk rather a lot. We had kippers for supper, very nicely cooked so they were soft and juicy. Stewed apples and custard after. You said to tell you. I know you don't like kippers but these were nice.

Were too.

After supper the principal had us in her office by houses. The college is a terrace of three houses joined together. I'm in the middle one. The kitchens are extensions fastened onto the backs. I can see their roofs from the corridor window. Miss Torman explained more about the ideals of Miss Manners and Miss Welbeck. We won't do any teaching practice till next term.

Please give Mummy my love,

with love from Kate

Upstairs at 16 Back Street, solid middle-aged woman, mother of a ten year old daughter, reading that stuff, felt hot. Why on earth had Daddy kept it? Why now—go on remembering?

Two stools. The light on of course, room still gloomy. Get him sitting.

Daddy—

Uhn.

Silence, on and on for ever. It seemed. What sticks, the sitting in that enclosed space, knowing it had to be done. Really up against it for the first time, no choice, no-one else could do it. *Daddy—*

Well, what is it, girl? Come out with it.

Nothing inside to hold up the shoulders.

School's not going to sack you, are they? His face telling nothing.

Course not, Daddy. Jelly lips and then, *Thing is, I've filled in these forms.*

Can always tear them up again.

This almost wail, shameful, bursting out, not what was wanted. *I've got to get your signature,* and him crossing one leg over the other and placing one elbow one the table, supporting himself on the stool. *If you could bring yourself to reveal to what, I'd know what to say.*

Daddy, but that lump of a girl with sweaty legs, perched on a slippery stool in a dark room, pushing feet down on the bar, knowing she'd said every last thing that was bound to rub him up the wrong way—*Daddy, I've applied to learn to teach Domestic Science.* And him not helping. *Who's going to pay for this?*

A miracle that innocent had taken in about grants. *You apply to the local authority—*

Doubt if they'll want to give me anything. Work hard all your life and make money. Great mistake. Never raise a finger and they're all over you. Dismissing his daughter the way Mummy dismissed him. No, playing a trout. Way he was. Aunt Peggy too. Stood back. Watched. *All the same, Kate, if that's what you really want—and I'm not surprised to hear it—pretty obvious, I'd say—though what your mother's going to say—*

She knows I'm stupid.

Don't you dare say that. Smiled at last—the startlement of it—and the warmth that came flooding with it. How things ought to be. *Now suppose you get down to telling me a bit more about this college.* Looking at him, realising he's still teasing, gabbling about London and The Manners-Welbeck Institute of Domestic Arts.

Him still dry, *Can't say I've ever heard of it,* and back to stuttering on, about Miss Taylor saying it's famous. *All over the world.*

If she says so. Is there a reason for the name?

The room with more air in it now. *Olive Manners and Amy Welbeck.* Battleaxes Marion called them. Well—Victorians, bit starchy perhaps and clever women always a dicey topic. Mummy different—good-looking. He said so. And of course he'd loved her. *You see, Daddy, they saw how badly fed a lot of children of poor families were in those days, explaining, Miss Manners lived in Norfolk and saw the homes of farm labourers. Miss Welbeck's father ran a Mission in East London. That's what made them think—some mothers managed in spite of everything. So how did they do it? Find out and train teachers so all the girls from poor families could know how to cook really good food and how to buy the best they could afford.* Gabbling on. Good place, the Institute. Sounds out of date now? Why? Food technology not the same. If only we still taught proper cookery.

Sounds very commendable. And this goes on today? In that new world now the war was over and everyone would have equal chances, this huge smile. *Well. I agree with you, Kate, I like food. So where's this form then? Happen to have it with you, do you?* Reached into his breast pocket, produced that gold fountain pen. A great big flourishing signature.

And that's a blackbird. Not the same as the one that sits on the stables. This one always on top of the cypress. They whistle to each other across the house. That was what was so odd about London. Quiet. Miles and miles of quiet houses.

Raining that day. Absolutely pounding down. Wouldn't have gone in else.

Didn't expect to love it.

Little mouse Kate. Fancy her having the guts. London that did it. Being in London, being put with Marion. Rock, rock, rock, rock...

Paddington, doors slammed, guards shouting, blowing whistles, steam blasting from funnels, people, people in all directions and get away from there—just the taxi gliding.

Gave him a tip. Terrified. He took it. Good beginning.

Damp yellow dough of fallen leaves. Three-storey terraces, porches, off-white pillars. Posh gone-off. Peeling brown board on two legs. Gold letters, faded, looking up at them for the second time, alone this time. So why Kate and not

Jenny—who'd seemed such a sure thing? *The Manners Welbeck Institute of Domestic Arts, founded 1893.* Nowadays Domestic Science. *Old-fashioned name,* Miss Carter holding out the admission form, *but up-to-date teaching. Very sound place. Couldn't do better.* Took it, filled in six passes at O-level —no need to mention the Fails and none of the passes up to much, except the one glowing, unwriteable 'Distinction' that no-one was supposed to know about because officially on the certificate there was only Pass or Fail but the school knew and secretly, against all regulations, they let on, this one distinction, that made it safe to apply. Pick up that suitcase, climb those steps, track down a bell.

Rock, rock, rock, rock and roll. What's that got to do with it? Runs in the head. But that place was always quiet. Even with crowds of us.

An echoing hall, flight of heavy brown stairs, brown linoleum, a door labelled Reception. Hands shaky again. Knock. Loud enough? Anyone answer? If not, what next? Marzie, wonderful Marzie. A smile behind a desk, *You are?*

Kate Lomas.

Ah, Miss Lomas—Who was this 'Miss Lomas?' For the rest your life? 'Miss Lomas'? Kate gone? New coat, too big, stiff. Very raw then. And if it hadn't been for Marion?

Mass of sandy hair. Not untidy. Just a lot of it. Bouncing into the room after the footsteps stopped. Room 34 M. Elgin, K. Lomas. That trunk in the centre of the floor, *Luggage in Advance, Miss Marion Elgin, The Manners-Welbeck Institute of Domestic Arts, 44-48 Maxine Road, London N3.* Two photos on one of the chests of drawers. Serious looking people. Not too desperately smart. Patchwork pyjama case shaped like a teddy bear. Showed. which bed she wanted. Two chests of drawers, two cupboards, two small tables with bookshelves, window between them, Victorian spire with carved bobbles, sort of behind the plane trees. Roofs and chimneys. surprising number of trees in between; still a sense of the city going on and on.

Nearly caught toe on that trunk.

Pile of papers on the bedspread, *Timetable, Institute Regulations, Plan of the Building.* Marzie rattling them off. Pointed white fingers running down a list. *No 34, sharing with Miss Elgin. Second floor. Turn right, don't take stairs in hall—baize door can stick. Don't give in to its little games—firm push all it needs—don't go up the next stairs—don't miss small stairs in Middle House—middle of green corridor—end too far—up two flights, left, 34 just round the corner. Sorry no-one about help you—shouldn't have any difficulty.* So typical. Dear Marzie.

No. Clutch those papers, try to smile, pick up suitcase. *Thank you.*

Glad you've arrived, Miss Lomas. You're sure to be very happy here. The smile swept all over you.

Sitting on that bed. Footsteps. Those photos staring. Gilbridge undies wouldn't look much compared to what must be in that trunk.

Head going round and round. Marzie'd said it would be easy. But. Looking Glass world. Corridors switched directions—cream paper above a brown dado, sideways through the baize door, dado this side bottle green, a corner where dark red replaces green.

Look all round.

Appearing; not Red Queen though high heels, bright red lips, classy voice. *Hallo. Lost?* Head-up ring rattling it all off. *Middle House. First House. End House. Where you trying to get?*

34.

Middle House top floor. Very muddling. End House third but numbers with three in are in Middle. Makes sense, doesn't it?

Don't know. Even now.

Hair permed in a roll. *Marzie tell you to take the back stairs? Very sensible. Behind you there to your right.* Marcia Kendrick. Deputy Senior Student. Here early to help Freshers find their way round. *Anything you want, ask me. OK?* Not bad when you got to know her. Made DS seem classy.

Back stair narrow and uncarpeted, feet clattering. Corridor with green carpet. Miss M. Elgin, Miss K. Lomas. The right to go in.

Marion bounced in. Always bouncing. *Come on Kate, don't sit there.* Rock, rock, rock, rock and roll. Record-player at full tilt and her bent forward, arms going. feet pounding, rock, rock and roll, *Off your backside, Kate.* And did, stand up. Not going at it like her, letting the rhythm get in all the same, lift, run everywhere, though not easy with it like her, going at it all the same beginning to feel different. Not that first day. Just sat looking. *I'm Marion. What does the K. stand for? Marzie give you the gen, did she? Can see it, there beside you, load of junk. Threw mine away. Find your way up here on your own?*

Nod.

If you can do that, can do anything.

Her kneeling beside the trunk, flinging up the lid. *Good omen. If you can do that—I got lost twice—had to ask and then didn't really understand—something about three houses—Well—one day*—Made you feel better. Always did. A card last Christmas. Can't imagine she'd be quite the same now. The pair of us dancing in our room, the record player, *Rock rock, rock rock, rock and roll. Don't just sit there Kate.* Those were the days. *Jungle dancing—what my teachers called it.* Her grin. *Silly old baskets.* Kate Bush tinny compared to that. How can Jo like her? Different times?

That first day. *Think I can get this stuff out of this trunk?* Sitting back on her heels staring into the depths, leaning forward beginning to pick clothes, books, shoes, stockings, slips out of the trunk, holding them up and looking at them, dropping them on the floor, not entirely at random, not according to any scheme possible to make out either. Sitting back on her heels surveying the mess, *The worst's still to come.* Not looking all that upset.

Like me to help? Me speaking like that to a stranger. Soon not. Gilbridge, Newcastle. Where she lived. Seemed so romantic. *Daddy was up that way during the war, something very hush-hush,* The romance of it shone round Marion's head.

Goes shooting? Hit many, does he? and giggling at her, that sourness—killing for fun—swept aside, *A terrific shot.*

Cor blimey, chum—whadya know? both accents exaggeratedly fake. No point trying to keep up with that.

Looking out that evening for the first time at the lights of the houses in the next road, pulling the curtain across the window, sitting down at that small table in room 34 to write a letter. Thinking there was a good chance he wouldn't show it to Mummy. *Domestic Science. What any sensible girl would want to do, Kate. Don't mind your mother.*

She pushes herself away from the balustrade. Ought to get on. But her fingers are still resting, the rough stone fitting into the unevennesses of worn skin while she goes on gazing at the garden. In better nick now than when she and John took over. Mummy never bothered. Neither Mummy nor Daddy at home much so the bottom end a wilderness. Wonderful place for a child but order has to be restored. What a garden's for. But a natural order, gentle not forced. So now, check if Pete's cleared the pond of blanket weed. She turns slowly left, pulls her fingers off the balustrade.

Wonderful, peaceful routine. White overalls for the kitchen, skirts and cardigans for lectures, brown overalls in the labs. It all made sense and was calm—kitchens with the cupboards all labelled, bowls, saucepans, knives shining, each in its own place. Everything we learnt fitted in, how to bake, stew, the difference between roasting and braising, principles of nutrition, hygiene, how to organise a classroom, how to calculate costs, time procedures. Hygiene. Blouse fresh in the morning, black line round the collar by evening. Woe betide the student whose blouse wasn't immaculate every morning. Day after day, endlessly washing and ironing. Look immaculate in a grimy world. These ancient battle-axes.

Observe Insti students, now teachers for real working in old buildings in dreadful, run-down parts of London. Hadn't ever seen such places but—shining kitchens, girls with their hair tied back, clean hands, rows of eyes gazing at the blackboard, then heads bent over their books. And then they cooked, a flush appeared in sallow cheeks as the room heated, they served up food with shining eyes. Or so it seemed that first term.

When you're there, look in the local shops. See what's available, what their mothers can find. See how much it costs. Best advice ever, Learn shop workers poor, dockers when in work, rich by local standards, standards not the same everywhere, money spent as it came in and in some families not much came in. Looked in all the corner shops—Camp coffee, sterilised milk, condensed milk, white bread, a few tired potatoes, a wilting cabbage, red jams, yellow jams, a slab of mouse-trap from which the shop-keeper cut smaller portions. Streaky bacon. Those sausages, had to be exactly quarter of a pound, bought from a local butcher to bring back to college. *Find out how much fat, how much sage, what proportion of bread-crumbs, how much meat. Think, think, what's available? What are the kitchens like in some of those flats? Think, how to help girls in those circumstances, how to lead them out into a wider world, how to ensure their children are better nourished.*

Hard but wonderful. Even teaching practice. Some of those girls were wild. Never really came to terms with them—didn't know enough, shy country girl—others didn't care—they knew how to live, didn't they? Their mothers knew all about it and this stuff all fancy nonsense—but many solid, sensible, reliable. Watching them carefully as they broke eggs or stirred, thinking they'll make something of their lives.

She turns right at the end of the terrace, greets the scent of the bay, stops. The tulips in the bed under the house are going over, can still make out they're too blue to be pink, too pale for more than the tips of the petals to be purple, tall, very pure shape. Probably planted by the Ardens. Sense of time going back. She checks her watch.

Marion'd sing mornings—and in the common room after lunch and in the meeting hall in the early evening before supper and weekends. Never missing a chance. *Rock, rock, rock, rock, rock and roll.* Oh she was mad.

Not bad to be mad at that age.

Other days it was hymns; knew some of them from school. A good voice, Marion's, though not as sweet as Sheila's. Put more into the words. *Yea, though I walk through the valley of the shadow of death*—Still wonder now—if—

Never heard of some of them—

Let all mortal flesh keep silent

and in fear and trembling stand,

to a delicate and tremulous tune

as the light of lights descendeth

and the darkness clears away.

Humming in corridors and all sorts of unsuitable places. Including words, coming back time after time, whatever they meant. Good to clear away darkness. Though how? And what? Doesn't change. Still a mystery. Last week Mummy insisted it was Thursday when it was Saturday.

There's the pond. And it's clear. Water looks good. Mummy's room faces south-east. Sun still here this afternoon but moving off. The cake will brighten it. *The chairman will cut the cake* and Mummy moving the tip of the knife to the exact spot for the first thrust. As if it mattered to her.

White icing shines up and a ring of candles. Still a few minutes left for the pond.

Early afternoon. Which had been hard to believe in that grey light. Pond with concrete edges, but a few mallard. Seven to be exact, three drakes, four ducks. Fancy remembering that. And—in this London park with all that dull grass—pair of goalposts but no boys kicking a ball—wild ducks—sculling up hopefully but all the same, wild. At Holmbush some michaelmas daisies would still be out, bronze chrysanths on the second terrace.

Not that the Institute wasn't wonderful, from the word go more or less, but—an open place, trees, grass and pond with mallard. Not a sound anywhere, wind blowing through and being there alone. Not that anyone at college interfered, all the same an unpressured place, like the garden at Holmbush, that garden the reason perhaps why it was impossible to stay in London at the end of the course—coming down from the platform in high heels holding that diploma, still rolled up now in its holder at the back of the third drawer, no need to insist on it now—but came back to the countryside that was built in, built in, yes—but not—maybe, perhaps, someone else might say—not to somewhere close under Mummy's nose.

She examines the pond. Pete's done a good job. She can see the mud on the bottom and dark red, crumpled water-lily leaves not yet risen to the surface. Yes, the school in Fairhurst, digs in Gilbridge, becoming part of St. Mark's, a life she stares at now, lived more under Mummy's nose than she'd thought, but quietly, quietly. She takes another look at her watch.

The rain wasn't much at first. So lingering, watching the ducks. The sheen on the drakes' necks as vivid as on those of the pheasants under the plum-tree at Holmbush. The rain soon made itself felt. By the gate, pouring. No gabardine. Why not? Young don't think. Jo no better, worse if anything. None of them nowadays believe rain makes you wet.

Uphill towards the Institute a real blast of wind and rain. Drips from hair down back of neck. No sign of a bus. Ridiculous any way to take one for such a short distance. That church clear to see every day from room 34. Sort of friend really, becoming one anyway. Sheila'd said churches always open in case people wanted to pray. Didn't want to pray—*disgusting superstition*—no idea how to set about it, but if the place would keep anyone dry?

Struggle to get that door open, not that it fought back, more as if it felt its weight and needed time. Yes, that's true —even after to someone who's known them for years, a church door still has the feel of opening to something that has to be come to slowly, a walled garden, with its own ways.

Row after row of brown pews—and no idea yet how agonising they could be after an hour or so sitting. Gawping there in the greyness. Rain always made the place dark: avenue of round pillars, distant roof crossed by branching beams, windows whose reds and greens were black like antirrhinums and peonies in late evening, the scent of flowers—arum lilies a long way off up there in huge brass vases at opposite ends of the altar, covered with an embroidered cloth. Came to love it later—got up from knees at the altar and there, below the white cloth spread over everything for Sunday, gold-thread flowers. Another scent too, faint, metallic. No idea then what it was. Or did a word drift in—frankincense, frankincense and myrrh, words murmured year after year after the carols at school at Christmas? *That superstition wrecked your grandfather's life.* He slipped you his prayer-book. Not long before he died.

Flummoxed by that brass eagle, feeling the ridges of the feathers, goodness knows why. What could that tell a lump of a girl standing at the chancel steps wondering whether that enormous bible might not slide off, crash if she touched it, suspecting even then, that not the right question, scared someone'd walk in and catch her? Only in there of course to keep out of the rain. Still pouring. Back and forwards to door.

Had to do something so try a hymn book? Knew a lot of words from school. Sheila singing them, and Marion. Didn't seem to have done them any harm. Marion different from people in Fairhurst. Peculiar? Certainly not. Friend? Definitely and home miles away.

There at All Saints each Sunday with her. Only trying to find out. Mummy said everyone should think for themself, see what was wrong with things for themself. Convinced they'd see it her way.

Only it seemed good.

She leans toward the pond. That grey oval floating just underwater is the foot of a watersnail walking upside down clinging to the underneath of the surface, a dull jelly all it shows to the upper world, not very attractive, hiding itself between glinting angles of light and in its shell. That's natural for a snail. *Weaklings who creep off to hide in religion.*

Used to hide in the garden. Weak, probably, and this weakness a built-in bias time after time toward the singing, the embroidered vestments, the colour, the uncanny lingering scent of incense, the strange words, the rituals that had been performed that same way for centuries? Becoming part of the ages, not alone drifting in an alien world, not shown up as stupid. In church nobody's perfect—all we like sheep—forgive us, Lord—so no worse than anyone else. Or not much.

People were friendly; glad, they said, to see a young face. Yes, young then and not wanting to hurt Mummy. So saved up to get her a nice warm scarf for Christmas. Did too, mohair. She said it was very nice but the loose wool would irritate her skin. Nothing to give her today, only the cake. She checks her watch again and turns toward the kitchen, stops under the arch. Very early in the year for roses but here they are, buds on the Yellow Canary, some already half open. It's been a warm spring. Here's something for Mummy, nothing very much, just an offering from a garden she's missing so much. She never admits to anything of course but how could anyone not miss all this? She must be pining. She breaks off a first twig, gathers a small bunch.

12.37 p.m.

As she passes the kitchen window, Jo notes Mum's not there. She slips in, grabs a bowl, the packet of cornflakes—Gawd, I'm ravenous—drowns them in milk, fills the kettle, switches on, leans back against the work-top and stands there gulping them down. She selects the mug with scarlet poppies, makes coffee, while she's at it grabs a sandwich, turns toward the door her hands full of mug, bowl, sandwich.

'Where are you taking those, Jo?'

'Upstairs.'

'You know you don't take food all over the house.'

'Oh mum,' She keeps her back to this voice that's suddenly taken over the kitchen. 'Look, I'm totally, absolutely famished.'

'You'll spoil your appetite.'

'Not a chance, Mum, not a chance. I could down an elephant.'

'I made those sandwiches for our lunch. And just look at you, you're filthy.'

What would anyone expect? She tries to balance her load in one hand while reaching for the door with the other, but Mum can be so pig-headed.

'Wash your hands and come and sit down.'

Jo feels the long muscles in her back tauten, hesitates, she really can't manage all this lot at once, wearily gives in. Her mother turns the tap onto the lettuce, throws words over her shoulder. 'Have a nice ride?'

'Fine.'

'Sharon with you?'

'Mmm.' Jo bites fiercely into the sandwich.

'How's she?'

'Fine.'

'Nice girl.' She starts spinning the lettuce in that funny plastic basket.

Jo considers her back. 'I'm not coming.'

Her mother reaches into a cupboard for glass dish, places it beside her on the drainer, empties the lettuce into it. Jo's spoon scrapes on the bottom of the cornflakes bowl. Her mother's voice emerges backwards, through her head. 'Go upstairs and get washed and while you're at it, put on something decent. Then we'll talk.'

Jo stares round. It's horrible the way everything in this kitchen looks so smug. That silly row of mugs. All those painted carrots and toms. She pushes her chair back so the legs grate on the tiles. 'Made my mind up.'

Once upstairs she puts on Kate Bush. as loud as possible though it doesn't suit that voice but Mum won't know that and she only wants to drown everything out, to send that sound surging out into the world so everyone can hear even if Kate Bush sounds like a witch, a banshee, all the better if she does, that's the magic of it. *Let me in, let me in, let me in.* She wants to be in that house with Heathcliff. He's the centre of her life; it doesn't matter what anyone thinks, with him she feels real. And how can anyone feel real when their best friend's given up on them, totally deserted them and they've been friends all their lives and now they've been left alone, in a world where homework's the realest thing, piles of it after school cutting them off from a pony who really needs them and it's all nag, even down to telling them what to wear—*not those tight jeans, not those platform sandals*—not wanting a person to be themself, moulding them shapeless with a purple blazer with a crest on the pocket, trying to force them into the darkness of that house in Gilbridge. If there was anything they could do in a place like that it would be different. But there isn't. Absolutely isn't.

She leaves the door open so she can still hear Kate Bush from the bathroom and steps under the shower. Warm water swooshes over her skin, swirls red round her feet, the stickiness which she hadn't noticed till now, has gone. She sways, allowing this warm silk to caress right shoulder then left, breasts, stomach, thighs, plunges her head into the flow, feels it's fingers running over her scalp, her hair smoothing and dripping.

By the time she's back in the bedroom, the music's stopped. She puts the disc on again, tears open a drawer, pulls out the hip-length green and blue check blouse. It's got its points. Not the old jeans. Flares are completely utterly out, though according to Mum this pair's too good to throw out. Doesn't mean you have to wear them. She puts on the pair with straight legs. the new pair of high-heeled boots. *One has always thought of boots as things to wear out of doors.* She inspects the smooth the line over her legs with the jeans tucked into the tops. Even if all a person's doing is going to is an Old Folks' Home, which she's not, they want to look with it.

'Jo, you ready, Jo?'

Not bloody likely. What Meg said yesterday, not quite aloud but we all heard and Miss James didn't quite, though she suspected.

She puts on the disc for the third time but this time turns down the sound so she can hear the mystery, how it seems to come from a distance, calling. She gazes out of the window. The soaring point of the cypress remains dark and still. She turns back into the room, jiggles her hips a little, picks up her comb, The voice streams round her but now she can't get into it. She frowns at her face in the mirror. They think you don't know a thing when you can see clearly as anything. Why can't Mum grasp Gran isn't into birthdays?

That horrible house and that watery voice. *I want to go to Andover.*

Gran herself. Talking about when Mum and Dad got married. Said January when it should have been June and a minute later said Aunt Peggy wasn't there when there's a photo shows her lined up with the rest of them. *Accuracy is of the essence.*

To go to that house is to enter a darkness where things hang in the air, they're totally not right and there's nothing you can do. She won't go.

What makes her all the more determined is the sight of a box that's got to hold that stupid cake, plonked there in the middle of the table in case they might forget it. Not much chance of that. Mum flustering about. For heaven's sake, she's got out all last year's jams and is wiping the shoulders of the pots with the dishcloth. Hasn't she got anything better to do? Fiddle, fiddle, why can't she sit quiet?

Her mother runs her eyes over her, tightens her lips. 'I'll put these away later. We'd better eat.'

Why? There's no hurry. But she's still a bit hungry.

'Here, we'll try one of these chutneys.'

All the times she's eating Jo keeps her eyes on the table. When it's all finished she raises her head, starts to push back her chair.

'Where you going? Don't get involved in anything. We're leaving in half an hour.'

Jo grits her teeth.

'Gran's eightieth birthday,' Mum says, wheedling.

Does she have to stare like that?

'Look, Jo, we've had this out before. Her big day. You're not eighty every day, you know,' and then her voice drops; there's a threat—but it can't be—of tears in it. 'Jo, I need you to come.'

Jo shrinks back, clasps her hands, stares down, at last growls up with. 'You can cut the cake without me.'

'It'll make a big difference if you're there.' The voice artificially warm. 'Gran'll be so pleased.' Won't care one bit. 'You mean a lot to her.' How possible? Only me. Nothing great.

She challenges watching her face, 'You mean she pays for me to go St. Anne's. You didn't want me to go.' Enjoys the wince.

'Water under the bridge. It's her birthday, Jo.' She leans forward and Jo sees into her eyes, the real truth she's hiding. 'It's that house, isn't it, that horrible house and that ghastly old hag?'

'What ghastly old hag?' But it doesn't ring true. 'Don't talk like that. It's not kind. She can't help it.' She knows exactly.

'I heard, you and Dad, I know what you were saying.' Mum can't answer. 'Gaga, off with the fairies, shouldn't be there. Other places more suitable for people like her. Only got to that house because her brother's on the planning committee.' She watches her mother's face. 'Wheels within wheels, that's what Dad said and you said nothing'—just like she's silent now. 'He knew her years ago, tried to help her Dad tie her money up so that her brother couldn't get to it but he was too clever.'

'For heaven's sake, Jo, I never thought you'd be capable of eavesdropping like that.'

Can't not hear things like that, or afterwards, get them out of your mind. 'Couldn't help it, could I? I was coming downstairs and you were going on in the sitting-room not trying to keep your voices down.'

'You still shouldn't have listened.'

'Get real, Mum,' and suddenly she leans forward into her mother's stillness, 'I'm only telling you to show I understand, She's ghastly, on and on about, *I want to go to Andover*,' and as she speaks, it comes to her from nowhere, pointlessly, Gran—that Saturday afternoon Mum insisted they had to go over to Holmbush to help her choose what things to take with her—Gran looking at the wedding photograph of the family, pointing to Great Aunt Peggy, saying to Mum she was *some sort of cousin of your father's. One never knew her very well.* Mum's face flattening.

'That place doesn't make sense.'

Suddenly her mother smiles. 'You can say that again.' Her hand creeps across the table, 'So you'll come, Jo?'

Twenty minutes later with that box in her arms. 'I'm going now to get the car out, Jo.'

'Hold on a second, I'm coming.' Keep your hair on, don't get in such a tizz.

5

1.49 p.m.

Lunch has finally dragged to an end, Alice, with an effort, is back upstairs, her room, thank goodness, in the correct place. She closes the door behind her, hobbles to the centre table, lays the envelope she's carrying firmly on it. There, that's it. She remains glaring down. *The custom of the house.* That one becomes the target of eyes. All of them round the table staring. *Happy birthday* and *Do open your card,* yellow roses in a silver vase and that ridiculous singing.

A blank opens in her mind through which words float in, *Thou hast conquered, O pale Galilean—*

Her face creases, That was not—not what—not what had been there; that was something else—that was forced on one, like politenesses. One mouthed them—didn't one? Surely one did. About—?

About a birthday, as if a birthday meant something. So absurd. It only marks that one was once born and now is older. Happens without effort, achieves nothing. They wear one out with these *celebrations*, these normal people.

Mother enforces normality with curling tongs. Searing heat close to the cheek. *Stand still, Alice. Happy birthday, Alice. Nice children* brought in specially *to play with you.* Mother's curling tongs. *You must learn to behave nicely in company, Alice. The custom of the house.* One mouths curling tongs

She becomes aware she's standing in the middle of the room, shifts her feet, considers the bed, decides on the chair. The old always sleeping. Granny used to sleep. Mercifully. But first there's something to find. That thing. That Miss McDonald has hidden in the room. Where is it? Must find it. She hobbles at top speed to the corner inside the door. Not there. So where? She looks wildly round. Impossible to hide it behind the bed. The bureau touches the bookshelves. She makes her way to each corner in turn, pulls the curtains aside, peers under the table. And people are coming. One can hear them talking, outside somewhere. One must go to meet them. She opens the door, sets off as fast as she can down the corridor. Where can they have they gone? Here are stairs. They must be down there. At the turn of the stair the pot of ferns catches her eye. She pauses. Perhaps they're in there, hiding among the leaves. She starts to search them with trembling fingers. *What makes you think you're going to Girton?* Mother's arranging roses in the scullery. Blowsy pink roses with a heavy scent. *If you were a boy—*

Hurry up and finish. There's the silver to polish. She searches again. There's no silver in this vase.

'Mrs Lomas, is something the matter, Mrs Lomas?'

She straightens, gazes uncertainly at the face confronting her. 'They're not there.'

A pause, then, 'No they're not.' A hand reaches towards her, hovers, doesn't touch. 'You look tired. Shall I help you back to your room?'

Alice nods. It's all one can do. She starts to climb the stairs with that beige skirt beside her.

The skirt eases her into her room, plumps up the cushion on her chair. 'There you are.'

Alice subsides into it, relaxes and gazes up. Her eyes focus. 'Thank you Miss McDonald. One can manage.'

'Naturally you're tired. Try to get a little rest. Before your family get here.'

Family? Alice stiffens.

'A rest makes a lot of difference.' The voice is gentle, soothing, almost smothering like beige flannel. One has to submit.

And she goes.

Not that one will sleep, not after this—one had supposed among strangers there'd be peace, all one requires is peace, not this circle of voices. *Do open your card.* She lowers herself, adjusts her shoulders, sits straight. Gradually the cube—walls, floor, ceiling—asserts its calm. The lids slide down over her eyes.

Fat yellow roses, prone to drop; scent and cold damp. Missionary and missionary's wife. Cold damp in the scullery. Silver fish under the sink. Two glass vases on the draining board, large pair of scissors, tough stalk between the thorns. *Make a good long slit, Alice. They need to drink.*

Parched, parched.

Put in some of this gypsophila.

Yes, mother, but one is parched, wilting. She opens her eyes, gazes hazily at the room, listening to a voice, there in the scullery behind her.

Why don't the teaspoons wear away with polishing? One doesn't polish silver fish,

I don't know how I've let everything get so behind hand. It was your father being called out for Mrs Emmings.

Echoing up. *Mrs. Emmings* in the distance, knocking against damp walls.

He was with her all day yesterday. Poor woman. They wanted him there at the end but it threw everything out and he'll have the funeral, early next week, they say, when her sons can get here. So for this evening, Ella can deal with the vegetables but I'll have to do the pastry. She has a heavy hand. You can see to the apples.

Yes, Mother. This is clear now, the meal already sour in the mouth—and the mere thought of the conversation. But one tries. To meet her half-way. A waste of time and effort. One imagines by Monday she'll be grateful. It is not reasonable to imagine.

One doesn't keep one's mouth shut. One asks them to follow reason. All that's needed, so simple.

Like taking one's turn with Granny. *Simple. Just be on hand in case she needs the WC. Remember to take her lunch in at one.* Granny puts her hands in the gravy.

Mother's picking at a piece of fluff on the slim curve of her skirt. *School work, you mean? I can't imagine why they don't let you have your holidays in peace. It's not as if it matters.*

Words flow freely now along grooves in a well-worn record.

It does matter.

My dear, of course you must do your lessons, but just now, let's get on with the silver, shall we? She comes three steps closer, adjusts the collar of one's blouse. A noose tightening. *There, that's better.* One's gasping in the sickly perfume of her soap. She taps three times lightly on the shoulder. *Of course it does, dear, but not as much as you think. Perhaps you could bring yourself to face the fact this is your life you're living now.* One dreary corridor of furniture to be polished, silver to be cleaned, flowers to be arranged.

But, mother, I'm going to Girton.

What makes you think that?

Father—

Your father loves you very much but he doesn't always face facts—he can't afford it and you're needed here.

She has no business attacking him.

If there'd been a boy—of course that would be different. As it is, you'll have to knuckle down, Alice. Stop giving yourself airs. Mother pulls herself up. *Do be sensible, dear, I know it's hard—but it's what comes to all of us. Do you think I wanted to end up as rector's wife in a backward little place like Ferdington?* She sighs, clasps her hands. *It's in your own best interests. You'll see that in the end. You'll want a home of your own one day and no man wants a wife cleverer than himself. You don't want to end up as a dowdy little school teacher in some dreary little school. What kind of life's that?*

The sun's still streaming in. The smell of roses hangs in the air. Mother throws her head back, walks out. A voice calls, *Where you going, Muriel? Get back in your room.* Coarse local accent. *I told you to stay there.* From the head of the stairs.

Tall stair and one's looking up. *I told you*—The pitch of that voice. Impossible not to hear. Stair with dark banister; one's standing at the bottom.

Quick. Into the study. Quiet in here with father, sitting at his feet beside a strong brass fender, punched with a trefoil pattern, with knobs like baked apples, a tiled hearth. Mother hates those tiles. *More suitable for a bathroom than for a priest's study.*

But here she is, in here where she never comes, in the middle of the room, clasping her hands, dark blue skirt swinging a little, Father smiling, gently so he must be trying to calm her down. And now she's turning her eyes away, retreating towards the door.

Alice's frown eases. She shifts her foot, raises her head, gazes round the room. That's father's bureau. Those are the curtains one chose for the sitting-room at Holmbush. Here in the armchair one's inclined to sleep but blue sky's crossed by window bars. Their shadows slanting.

The web. Stretched across the right-hand bottom light of the high classroom window. All the threads straight. The web looks round but when one really stares all the edges are straight. Would like to touch but Miss French is looking. Each of those sections is a parallelogram. Not a rhombus. Miss Mathematics says a rhombus has four sides but all slanted. It's there in the book. These lines face each other, two parallel, two slanting. Could show her the web, *Each of those sections is a parallelogram.* One doesn't do that. It's showing off. The spider weaves geometry by nature. Maths underlies the world. *Sorry, Miss French.* What was she saying? *Le pupitre, la porte.* Words differ in English and French but

French spiders must weave the same way as English. The steady, reliable logic of nature.

Get back into your room. I told you to stay there. Those voices shatter logic.

At the foot of the stairs, looking up at the two of them. Mother's bottle green skirt dark against the walls. Day after day. *Your turn to look after granny, Alice.* Ella says, *Lock her in.*

'I'll take over, Mrs. Hebden.' A voice that runs on softly. One has seen her placing a hand on an arm. 'Can I help you, Miss Ingram? Where do you want to get to? Always so many places to go, part of life's journey I think. Here I am, twittering on and you want to go somewhere. I'm sorry, not Andover. I know how you love it—must be a wonderful place—but it's too far away today. Let me find you your room.'

So it's not surprising to hear another knock on the door. She starts, refuses to open her eyes, hears the door open, knows it's Miss McDonald again, popping in. 'So sorry to disturb you but your daughter'll be here quite soon.'

Alice eyes her. Another excuse to insinuate that thing?

'She's always so punctual. Just wanted to make sure you're all right.'

Alice raises heavy eye-lids. There's nothing in her hand. Though outside the door? That beige the woman insists on wearing, an undistinguished, bad-tempered colour. Mother wears a coat in a shade she pleases to call camel, a nasty-tempered creature if ever there was one. *It suits me,* she says and who is one to deny it? Beige more malleable, expresses Miss McDonald's mind. Perfectly. She has no sense of sequences, apparently doesn't aim at logic. An undistinguished mind, shapeless,

She makes the effort to sit up straight. Lines sink down between her eyes. Although honesty is of the essence, an elegant moment should be found for making things clear, and one should remember that not everyone's had one's own intellectual advantages. She smiles graciously. Now now, Alice, try to think of her good points. For someone whose only training is nursing, Miss McDonald's not too impossible. After all she's so far avoided that symbiotic questioning one so dreaded, relating to 'our' movement this morning. One should give credit where credit is due.

Miss McDonald babbles on. She hopes, is concerned, thought at lunch—maybe—says it all means nothing, hopes again.

What? And what's this, about *your daughter*? 'Kate?'

'About three, she said. Bringing Joanne.'

'Of course.' Who else would she bring?

'They're so looking forward to seeing you.'

Alice serves up her best ice. 'And I shall be delighted to see them.'

Miss McDonald moves toward her. 'Of course,' stands a moment, half smiling, half frowning, turns away, turns back, face full of creases. 'Are you all right?'

'Naturally.'

After a minute's pause the release comes, 'I'll leave you then.'

Best thing she could do but even after the door's closed behind her, she's made it impossible to settle. The sun's gone off this chair, a bus is huffing outside, intrusive forms are moving in the room.

Alice's face tautens, she stretches her legs, waits, then suddenly relaxes. It's cosy here sitting beside the fender at his feet.

Don't let Alice disturb you, Edward.

She's no trouble. Fact is, she helps me concentrate, sitting there quietly thinking her own thoughts, and he smiles. She goes and the two of us are left alone now, all peaceful and quiet under the gaslight.

His shoulders are square against the ceiling. The light's a halo round his head.

One's finger is tipped with black.

He smiles down. *Use the corner of your pinny.*

The cotton's pure white. *A little piece of paper. Can you find one, Father?*

He laughs, but softly, the curls on his beard stand out in the gaslight, a huge hand descends offering a scrap of *The Church Times. Little Miss Finnicky.*

How many times have I told you to keep your fingers off those tiles? Anything that needs thought is anathema to Mother but we've got rid of her and the finger traces the way lines cross, weave in and out, make patterns that need time to work out, triangles, octagons, squares, sequenced and overlapping, narrow lines tracing their edges. One can go for a journey, find routes, discover how each line returns at last to through the same series of patterns to the same place, the end—or new beginning—it had to reach. What's it matter if the finger that's done all that has collected coal-dust and Mother'll stare as if she's seen a spider? She tells off Ella for shrieking at them.

Father wants to understand. *What were you doing?*

All tied together, all the way across. He's looking, frowning a little but not angry. *The lines—edges—lines running round the edges*—words can't find a way—*the lines all fit and some of the shapes fit back to back and others fit across on top of them.* That's it. Keep the hand with that finger in the air, above the tiles not getting dirty. There was a man here who spread a cloth on the floor and left it spotless.

Do you like them? His voice is warm. He presses his hands onto his knees, stands, goes to the long shelves behind his desk, searches, finds it at last at the far end, crammed into the corner by the door, not one of his great, massive dark blue books with that complicated spider's web writing—He says it's German and he can read it. No-one else can round here. Mother can't, Ella can't, the organist can't, the churchwardens can't, no-one can except him, all those heavy navy blue books too heavy for one to hold but Father can read them and rich sounds flow.

He takes down a battered old book, coming apart at the spine, lifts one onto his knee. His beard tickles one's cheek. He opens the book, finds a page. *This is what those patterns are made of—look.* Four small squares make one big one, a square contains two triangles, or four. Trace them in the book with a finger. They all fit, can be placed inside and outside each other.

He turns the page. *Look, parallel lines. D'you see, Alice? They can never meet.*

A pair of lines snake out, circling the world. Only air holds them apart. *Won't they ever wobble and bump into each other?* One's very small sitting here by the hearth and Father's haloed by the gas-lamp. *Never.*

Alice suddenly opens her eyes.

Suppose they do?

Then they're not parallel any more.

She eases her shoulder against the chair, closes her eyes, shifts the shoulder again. The ache fades but doesn't go away. Rationality is of the essence. But there are clouds from time to time; thoughts seem to dissolve into them. One is more sleepy than one used to be.

At the head of the stairs. One of them is shoved back and later the other storms downstairs into the study. *I can't stand it any more.*

That horrible old woman—she stares into his hardening face *I'm sorry, Edward—she's mad.* Mad, mad. It keeps echoing. It's the way she clenches her fists, thrusts her arms down over the folds of her dark red skirt as if strength might rise from the floor. *I'm sorry, Edward—but—facts—*

His voice is soft, *Dora—my dear—*

One's finger traces out patterns on the tiles. Here is sense and patterns that make the universe comprehensible. One grasps truth here and order.

I wouldn't say it if it wasn't the truth. Mother's voice comes through her cheeks. *She's completely gaga. You've got to face it, Edward.*

One's finger following the edges of triangles that contain squares and over and through it all interwoven circles.

My dear—

There are places she can go. Mad-houses, yes, lunatic asylums—I'm sorry but that's the truth, you believe in the truth. What other places can there possibly be for someone who smears toothpaste all over her hair brush?

He rises, places his hands on her shoulders, *My dear.* Figures shape themselves, skirt and jacket moving as they must, his voice gentle as always. *I understand. I really understand.*

Mother stares into his eyes. But one's not looking, not listening.

She is my mother. We have no choice, Dora. The fingers gripping her shoulders are placed in a rough, inaccurate triangle like wisps of charity.

Mother stands clutching the centre frill on her blouse. Its high collar will choke her. For a long time she says nothing and then she goes, closing the door carefully behind her.

As one's finger traces the patterns on the hearth, they settle and make sense.

She stares at the surround of this gas-fire in front of her now which doesn't relate to the shape of the fire itself. Why not? Why do the tiles have shepherds on them? What is one doing in a room with shepherds on the tiles? One's never kept sheep. Her fingers clench over the arm of the chair. For a moment she'd like to cry out. Then her eyes come to rest on the bureau. A good piece that, Father's, and Kate can be roped in to polish. She sits up. This is a problem that opens to reason. That metal base, the one a man mended this morning, has been inserted into a grate intended for coal.

Silence and yells. Sometimes the yells are Granny's, sometimes Mother's. The silences are addressed to Father. Triangles and parallel lines are never angry. Parallelograms construct a spider's web, geometry underlies the world. This is what one has to remember, always and everywhere, knowledge that rises out of the tangle.

Mother lets her emotions become too much. One's only a child but one learnt to speak calmly when Granny comes ranting, waving her arms, to display no feeling, turn one's back. She sees she's making no impression. One locks her in. She cries of course. The sound comes through the door. Logic says she has to be locked in. She burnt a table cloth; let a hot iron fall on it and left it. She picked it off the stove and put her finger directly on the hot surface. Stands screaming while the iron burns a hole in the cloth. Without rational mind, what is she? It is a child takes charge, gets her back upstairs, turns the key.

2.49 p.m.

As the door opens the sun's warm on their backs. The air that meets them feels damp, seeping round the soft, snuffly bulk of Mrs. Hebden, fusty old pillow—shouldn't think that, sort of thing the kids say but—in her case—and there's that ghastly hall gaping behind her. Upstairs really nice, good bright rooms but this hall—John had a point. *Good God,* that first day, staring round, *an Egyptian tomb.* Glum enough and those fussy tiles, stained glass, throwing red and green stains on the tiling. Cold with it.

Doesn't seem to be doing much for Jo. John would say, *Stop looking like a sulky blancmange.* You can't. She can be terribly strong-willed. Got it from where? Good parent wouldn't have allowed it to start?

Kate checks she's holding the box upright.

Mrs Hebden's ogling its content. 'Lovely,' and beady eyes gleam over the mounds of her cheeks. 'Real icing, are they, those violets? You must have quite a hand.' She goes on staring. Her mouth hangs slightly open. What will she find wrong?

'Have to be born with it.' The fat woman sighs. 'Still, it's the taste that counts, isn't it? Can't tell that by looking at it.'

Sounds as if she doubts it tastes of anything. And it's not talent. Just plain, dull slog. A real flair—that must be a wonderful thing. And now that woman's had her say about the cake, she's turned her attention to Jo's jeans. Laser eyes beamed at her bottom. Just let her say anything. Kate clutches the box and advances into the hall.

'Mrs. Barnes,' Miss McDonald pops up out of nowhere, 'how nice to see you.' Peculiar woman? Unusual might be better, or even, though that could be going a bit far, odd. A smile spreads across Kate's face.

'Lovely day for your visit. We always seem to be so lucky with birthdays in this house, pure chance, I suppose.'

Sometimes let her words roll round like steam in a bathroom but today, feet, keep shifting.

Mrs. Lomas such a grand old lady. Miss M doesn't know what it is, but Mummy does get her talking. Who doesn't? Mind's been so sharp, finds the rest of us very slow, still, from time to time, you know, wonderful—though—though —and throwing back of the shoulders, 'Really caught me out this morning, brought me up quite short, I can tell you.'

Miss McDonald sounds amazingly cheerful, not at all as if she's been slapped down, might even enjoy Mummy's way of talking. Kate goes on looking. The housekeeper has this strange habit of bobbing every time she runs out of things to say, as if she doesn't want to look stiff and starchy, afraid she'll turn into a hospital matron or something.

Just now she bobs to face Jo. 'So nice of you to bring Joanne.' She looks less odd when she smiles. Her eyes are still sharp. Kate keeps hers off those jeans.

Which are of no interest to Miss McDonald, not in comparison with a young face. That sets her off in an outpouring of gush which Kate can't find the means to interrupt. 'How lovely to see you, Joanne, wonderful of you to come like a breath of fresh air, especially when it can't be very interesting for you, but a real treat for all of us old fogeys in here, and your grand-mother, mustn't forget her on her birthday. She'll be so pleased to see you and you're company for your mother, too.'

For goodness sake, the poor child.

The poor child glances at Miss McDonald, at first her eyes slide away, then she raises her head, smiles with an amber gleam. 'All in the day's service.'

'Really, Jo—'

But Miss McDonald looks for a moment as if she would like to fling her arms round her or clap her on the back, but instead she throws back her head in a burst of laughter. 'Twice in one day. Your grandmother, then you. I can see it runs in the family.'

Kate stiffens. She looks again at the stairs. 'Perhaps—'

But all the time Miss McDonald's eyes have been darting about busy as dragon flies. Now they home in on the box. She peers through the cling-film. 'Look here, have you seen, Mrs. Hebden?'

Mrs. Hebden comes to life like a comatose bloodhound. 'It's what I was saying before you got here, Miss McDonald,' she remarks as if through adenoids. 'Mrs. Barnes' got a real flair for it.'

'A work of art. What do you think, Joanne? Your mother's very clever isn't she?'

Joanne nods towards her mother. 'There you are.'

'Don't be silly, I did a course. Nothing to write home about.' But in spite of her efforts she's still afraid her pleasure is showing and that's such a silly thing to be pleased at.

'How clever of you to choose violets.'

Hardly chosen—all she had wanted was to avoid roses, because Mother has that thing about pink roses, and what other colour could you make them in icing?

'Out of fashion today, but there's no harm in that, no harm at all in old-fashioned sweetness and charm but, you know,' Her voice drops confidingly and one hand flutters. 'I love those shy little flowers hiding under their leaves, purple, the colour of evening, you know, and wizards' robes.' She gives her audience a rapid look. 'I think some strange things, you know. It's the poet in me.'

Kate's been relaxing in the steam, but she sees Jo's eyes come back into focus with a dangerous twinkle in them and Miss M was so patient with Mother when she was difficult over those bookshelves. Fortunately Joanne manages something harmless. 'Well, we didn't ought to keep her waiting, did we?'

Miss McDonald's eyes glow, a spot of colour dances in her cheeks she turns again to Mrs. Hebden. 'Isn't it lovely to have someone young to visit us?'

All the same the gaze she directs is a shining needle.

'Jo,' Kate says sharply, 'we ought not to keep Gran waiting.'

But action isn't so easy. 'Of course not, Mrs. Barnes. You're so right.' The housekeeper calls in Mrs. Hebden. 'Isn't that what I'm always saying? Old folk left sitting in their rooms. Some people are so inconsiderate.' Her eyes swing onto Jo. 'That's why we like people like your mother so much, who arrive on time and don't make their relatives wait. Old people get so anxious and there's no need. Most unkind.' Suddenly she waves an arm, turning a little sideways. 'All the same—if you can spare the time—mind if I ask something?'

Kate glances at the stairs.

'There was one thing that disturbed me—something she said—nothing very much but I couldn't see where it came from—'

'It is sometimes difficult to follow her.'

'Don't worry, Mrs. Barnes. Mrs. Lomas is a wonderful old lady. We do like having her here. She's no trouble, and she keeps us all on our toes. It's wonderful at her age. All the same some of those little remarks of hers, can be disturbing.'

Kate knows her mother's capacity for keeping people on their toes. From that point of view she's almost permanently off hers. She considers the housekeeper's enjoyment again slowly but comes to no conclusion. She has met people whose reaction to her mother have been quite different from her own, but none differ as radically as Miss McDonald.

Miss McDonald frowns. 'This wasn't her mathematics and all that. That's just her. Can't hope to keep up with that.' She hesitates, seems to force herself to it. 'To be honest, she is sometimes a spot confused, seems to be not quite with it, you might say.'

Kate's face doesn't flicker. 'She's very easily tired nowadays. After all she is eighty.'

The housekeeper considers her slowly and eventually remarks, 'Well, there's one little problem you might be able to clear up. She was talking about a man with a gun.'

Warmth comes back to Kate. 'My father. He was a terrific shot.'

'Ah.'

'Belonged to a shooting syndicate. Used to bring home what he'd shot, pheasants. partridges, hares—you know.'

'Aah.' Her face relaxes though her voice is still dubious. 'Well if that's it.' Her smile spreads across them both.' And it's her day. We had a little ceremony for her at lunch-time for her, nothing very much, just a few birthday cards, possibly all the same it could have been a bit too much for her. I do hope it was all right. Probably she'll tell you all about it.'

Kate smiles vaguely. 'Yes, probably,' hesitates, bursts out, 'My father, you know—' she darts a glance at Miss McDonald's face, sees nothing but interest, blurts on—'got an MBE, services to armaments.' Give him the credit he deserves in this place where Mummy gets everything.

'Strange isn't it, the things you've no idea about? One of the things that's so fascinating about this job. He must have been distinguished.'

Kate throws her head back and smiles, a bigger smile than any that's come this morning. 'My grandfather founded this firm making components for small-arms—firing pins, little things like that, suppliers to Webley. My father was the oldest son. Took over the firm when his father died so in 1914 he stayed at home to look after the business—essential war-work. All his younger brothers were killed so at the end of the war he hadn't the heart to keep it on. Decided to shoot for sport only so he sold up and put the money into Lomas and Kirkley, you must have seen it in the High Street, very good position opposite the church, just plain Lomas at first of course—' She draws breath and eyes the housekeeper.

'Why ever didn't I put two and two together? Of course, of course. Lomas isn't such a common name. I always stop, you know, going past, and look in. Not that I'm a great one for field sports but those rods—so beautiful in their way. Those lovely grippable handles and the lines they make—such delicate curves you can hardly believe it—must be strong after all and the flies—so dainty though I can't imagine how the fish are deceived; those colours are so glorious.'

'He was brilliant at display, very neat handed.'

'So that's where you get it from.'

Kate flinches. 'Impossible to reach his standard. Sam Kirkley's not half as good—though he's not bad. Some of his efforts are really quite nice. He's the whole firm now. Old Mr Kirkley gave up last year—year before was it? Trades under the same name. Once it's made, you know—'

'They didn't give Mr. Lomas an MBE just for establishing a good business,' Miss McDonald says, smiling but dry.

'That was the Second War. He wasn't called up—d'you mind if I tell you all this?' She glances at the housekeeper, standing there in the hall to the left of the front door with the door to her office just behind her, white paint on which the beading marks out insistent rectangles. But this is a chance, just once, to give Daddy his due.

'I love knowing. Makes me understand so much. All the residents—old when you first meet them and you've no idea, no idea at all. What they've been. One of my friends—someone I was in hospital with, years ago but we're still in touch—found one of her residents had been an Olympic swimmer, way back in the Twenties. Now couldn't walk. Still had the medals.'

'Daddy had medals. And cups. A row of them. For target shooting. He was brilliant. Secretary for Gilbridge and District Target Shooting Club. Chairman too. Did masses of work for them. Used to shut himself away drawing diagrams. Those things that make you more accurate when you're shooting, bullets, you know, firing-pins, whatever. Wrote articles and all sorts. Then he'd go up to the range.' Is Miss M not really believing? Can't explain clearly enough. 'Never told me. You can't when it's fire-arms. Wouldn't have understood any way. Must have had contacts. To get real bullets to try things out. Perhaps. I don't know. Certainly when the war came they wanted him. Took him off to this very hush-hush establishment somewhere up north.'

'So you grew up without him?'

'Only when I was very small. Hardly knew him at first when he came back but later it was fine. Though he was never in the house much.'

'So Mrs. Lomas made her own life?'

'They both did.' She stands quietly contemplating the fact. Amazing how things suddenly make themselves clear. 'But when they gave him his MBE—I was scared, you know, silly but—afraid she'd refuse to go to the palace, but after she'd told him what she thought, about the Queen and all that, she got out her best hat and went.'

Miss McDonald smiles. 'I certainly wouldn't have expected her to be trotting off to the palace without a word. She has very strong views. As I said, she keeps us all on our toes.'

She takes a deep breath. 'But sometimes, you know, the surprises she comes out with, a little—off course you might say. Something—not quite right. I think you should be aware of that.'

Kate goes stiff. 'Mummy can be upsetting if you don't know her.' Her hand grips the side of the box holding the cake, the fingers flat, not able to close as they might over a talisman. She peers into the musty depth of the hall. They all seem to be parts of a clock that's running down. The feeling's not altogether unpleasant. Soon it will stop altogether and they'll go on standing till something happens to set it going again. The voice flows relentlessly on and on —her memory, perhaps, her own world, a little upset at lunch—tick—tock—slower and slower while all Kate's own concerns get caught up in the rhythm—flowers, cake; knife, candles; Jo's hair, her jeans; John's supper; tomorrow's lunch; Mummy upstairs, waiting.

What will she say about that? Kate's not sure she would enjoy hearing, but at least she seems to have permission to go. She turns again towards the stairs and this time the tableau breaks up and she's allowed through—though that brings no sense of elation. Every time she comes she's surprised by those stairs. So many of them and they're so dark.

2.53 p.m.

God, this place is a grave-yard. Can't move without your heels going clack. You wait for it to echo back but it sort of dies away instead. These wretched flowers Mum's foisted on me to carry. *Must always take flowers. Your Gran loves the garden.* Never heard her say so.

Fatty can't keep her eyes off the cake. 'Real icing, are they?' 'What's Mum getting tense about? 'It's the taste that counts, can't tell that by looking at it. Violets are all very well but I really love roses.'

'Lovely to see you,' and Mum jumps.

That dull suit. Fits well though. Like feathers. If only it was brighter Miss Mac would be a robin trilling along about nothing. No, robins say real things. Defending their territory or making love or something.

'Lovely, lovely lovely. Birthdays in this house.' Oh Gawd. 'So nice of you to bring Joanne.' *Verbal diarrhoea.* What Megan said about her auntie. *Mind wonderful for her age.* Can't believe it.

Dad said *Gaga. OK, Kate, not quite yet but heading that way.* Wasn't talking about Gran. I think.

Way Mum's absolutely gawping, if she doesn't look out she'll start nodding to keep up with Miss Mac. Down, up, whoo-oo. Sort of short curtseys. When she was young—

Less odd when she smiles, her eyes still sharp though. Mum's being tactful, not looking at my jeans. Accept facts, Mum. Don't you know times have changed?

Lovely to see you. Do I think so? *Breath of fresh air, old fogeys, your grand-mother,* ugh. Though not such a bad old cow really. 'All in the day's service.'

Laughter. And laughter. Eyes darting and now she's onto the cake. 'Look here, have you seen, Mrs. Hebden?'

Snuffle, snuffle through that pig nose. 'What I was saying before you got here.'

Work of art. Clever mother.

She thinks so. And her efforts not bad. *Violets.* Yuck. *The poet in her—*

'Jo, we ought not to keep Gran waiting.'

Pause.

Old people left sitting in their rooms. Something she said. Man with a gun? Oh, oh, Gran would. Throw you. Bet she said it on purpose. *Away with the fairies?*—Didn't mean Gran and never heard they had guns. Gawd. How keep a straight face?

No but they're hinting at things. Dodging. Edging away. As if they can hear far off creepy aliens crying, *Let me in, let me in.*

Floor stays solid. Kind of glow in it. This place warmer than you think. Friendly feel of walls. Thick kind of wallpaper, white but some dashes of colour. It's the floor really. When you look through those blue and red shadows the sun's throwing through the front door. Underneath them, purple grapes, each fruit rounded, rising from the surface of tiles, not on every other, more every fourth; a leaf on each of the ones in between, looking very natural but not quite, little too square as if it's been laid out carefully to make it fit inside, a stem twisting round from one to another joining leaves and grapes all way across the floor as far as the stairs and, I suppose, to the back of the hall. Standing on a vine while Mum goes on about Grandad, words twisting back. Holmbush. The shop. The firing range. Used to ask to go there but he said no. Think I could shoot. Just as well as Gran. Fun to try. Mum never even wanted.

She's going on and on. Forever. Buck up, Mum. Don't keep Gran waiting. You said. Not that its going to be all that fun. Get it over. Get back to Nutmeg. Waiting. He called to the other ponies.

'He was knighted for it after the war—*services to armaments.* I was afraid she would refuse to go with him to the palace but after she'd made her thoughts clear she bought a new felt hat and went.' Mum takes breath at last.

'We had a little ceremony for her at lunch-time for her, nothing very much, just a few birthday cards, but she seemed to enjoy it.' Don't be a wally—be ice crackling all over. 'I expect she'll tell you all about it.' Hope not.

6

2.54 p.m.

Didn't take you long to abandon Holmbush, George. You'd always proclaimed you loved it so much—and yet you could always take yourself off, shop, firing club, woods, river, anywhere you could bring friends home from for your good little wife to smile at. That was all they ever wanted. And to be fed, naturally.

They had names, of course, and conversation, if one chooses to listen to shooting tittle-tattle, cups won or an afternoon in the woods—ten pheasants, three hares, a brace of partners, ambits and pigeons not worth counting. Such were your triumphs. The women gossiping, patting their hair, simpering, flapping their hands, *Poor little me*—except for the colonel's mare neighing her conviction she knew better about everything than Lady—A—with an indelible perm—a-a-ambrose. And when they'd gone, your hand on one's shoulder, *Well done, old girl.*

Old girl. Old. Girl. There was once an article on fractals. Accepted by *The Journal of Mathematical Studies.* One held it in one's hands. Offered it for your attention. Your eyes popped as if a pack of wolves had charged into the room. *You wrote this? In this house?* Where else? *I suppose I should congratulate you,* the words died in a puff of air. You were bewildered. *A normal woman would love this house, love entertaining*—did one never tell you about Bath? *She'd love looking after her child. Oh and by the way, there's a brace of grouse on the hall table. Present from Bill Smith because he likes the shotgun I recommended. He and Emmy are coming on Friday. I'll put out the Chablis. Take care it's correctly chilled. An unusual girl,* you'd said. Why did one fail to perceive you somehow expected a normal *fuzzy little head* to sprout on one's shoulders the moment one said *Yes?* Is such a head capable of appreciating the exact temperature of your favourite wine?

You tried your best, perhaps, stuttering a few words of uncomprehending congratulation. Now you've turned up here, stop skulking in the hedge.

That's better. You're clearly visible so you can remove that expression. Why didn't one see? You gave yourself away by your look when one put out one's hand for the gun. And the way you expected *the jolly girl* to come trotting meekly behind you back to the firing shed. And one did. For some mad reason one did.

When we sat on the rug one had to ask you for help to get up, was obliged to hold out a hand. Your fingers were warm. One gave way to the physical.

That title, *Mrs?* Could that conceivably have counted? Surely not. One had stood up to mother.

It is perhaps conceivable one was beginning to suspect life was wasted in that school, not teaching, not opening minds but supervising silly girls, checking clumsily mended stockings, reprimanding wrong coloured hair ribbons, gritting one's teeth at their refusal to think.

Better places existed, schools where one might have met girls with minds. They would always be so few. Your fingers were warm. You smiled, saying *an unusual girl.*

Slip in the cartridges, release the catch with the first finger of the right hand allowing the cylinder to revolve, look straight at you. Stretch an arm the way you demonstrated, fix an eye on the sights, pull the trigger. Newton's Third Law comes to life violently against bone and muscle. Firm oneself against it five more times.

How thrilled you were when your freak of a wife presented you with a sandy-haired daughter. *Takes after Nasha.*

Average, as I said to your sister. *I try to be accurate.* Bang, bang, bang. You turning back grinning. Bang, bang, bang, round after round and the rock walls resonating. One can't think in a din. Leaves shake in front of the eyes, blown apart by hope perhaps? Always that gap between hope and outcome. Words came, disastrous but true, *You shoot accurately,* and your eyes ran over one like rain.

Figures swing round in a cloud. One thousand, nineteen hundred and thirty-nine—what's in the name of a year? 39 not 14 but it's the second time in a lifetime, a plunge into darkness. Filled the first time with the shrieks of a mad woman, Granny pounding her fists, wrestling against Ella and Mother. Father always out, taking Christ to the bereaved, the pews on Sunday lined with women in black. War is the total expression of irrationality.

He wasn't always out; his study was calm but he was beginning to stoop. *We have to think of Christ's sacrifice and trust God, Alice.* But his face lit up when he turned to reason. One spread out an exercise book, *Look, father,* showed him the week's work, *Full marks again? Well done. Alice,* and raising his head towards the window, his voice softening, *When the turmoil is over, all this will still stand firm. There's peace in a page of geometry and eternal truths.*

What did you use those truths for, George? For your addiction, wasn't it, drawings made in the back of the shop, experiments on the range, the run of the lab in Birmingham? You said proudly you'd sold the firm. Your brothers were dead so, in their memory you alleged, *no more armaments.* Of course not. Only bullets. The design of bullets. No wonder in 1939 they took you off to be a boffin. One supposes you were a good one.

War is a bath seen from below, tilted over the edge of half a floor, a crater, fire ripping through a terrace roof, flying dust and soot, blackened faces, bodies pulled from the ruins, ambulances, men with blood on their faces waiting while one stands for hours washing up mugs in a mobile canteen. Did you know this, George?

Without you the house expanded. One could have hidden there.

Muddle, unnecessary muddle—people running round trying to follow directives, civil servants with addled brains. Particularly on the subject of women. On no consideration could a female join the ARP and when they could after all —but not with the same status as men—the explosions would be muffled in training sessions in case the sound was too much for delicate ears. Did they imagine the Germans would be equally thoughtful?

A woman with a small child. Exempt. *Any normal woman would want to look after her child.* Mrs. Forster was a God-send

All those women in green uniforms running about, flapping their hands, *poor little me,* the colonel's lady taking charge, then standing back. One could sort things out faster: 1,500 pairs of girls' knickers delivered to the school in Iver St. Mary. Which has received only boys evacuated from Bethnal Green. Two parties of girls from Birmingham have arrived with brown paper for underclothes, one in Cardiff, the other in Pontypridd. Find a lorry with space, a driver, petrol, get them off, ring Cardiff, ask them to put up the driver overnight, tell them there are rumours of a twenty boxes of soap in Chelmsford, arrange for blankets for the boys to be picked up in Gloucester on the return journey. Day after day, *What do you think, Mrs Lomas?* Women in green uniforms coming with their need of First Aid training, of a car, shedding their silliness, learning to change wheels and sparking plugs, in small back kitchens making enough sandwiches to feed troop-trains, driving mobile canteens, finding a way round and through blocked roads, undeterred by shelling, becoming capable, rational. Did boffins have time to realise what was going on? One would suppose not.

Drop your arm, George. You're in the angle of the window, not on the range. It's too late to make a target of your wife now. Your fingers were warm then. One was beguiled. Which isn't rational. One should not be beguiled but you beguiled my daughter. *Don't be so hard on her, Alice. She's a normal, nice little girl.* Taking her off to the shop, filling her mind with your blather till all she wants is to be ordinary.

Skulking now are you? Like you sulked in your study all those years when you'd stopped being a boffin? One hardly ever saw you, only the stubs of your cigarettes left stinking out the hall. That's what one remembers you by, the absence of that reek. Every time one goes through the hall you're not there.

The way our feet bang on these stairs why don't they put down a carpet the whole house can hear us going up going up they can't hear us carrying that cake but it's as if the cake is shouting letting everyone know we're wasting our time and the sun's shining outside Nutmeg's alone in his field and we're going up these stairs past that plant which doesn't look like a real plant because its leaves are stained red and blue why does anyone put a plant where its leaves are going to be stained why does anyone put red and green glass in a window to stain the light that's coming through onto Mum's shoulders as she goes up carrying that cake up to a corridor of doors all of them covering boxes an old person inside each being shaped to fit and that old lady woman hag who wants to go to Andover which I don't know where it is but would absolutely love to tell her if only she'd go there

Mum knocking on Gran's door 'Come in,' and that's it, we've had it.

Love's what matters most. And understanding, understanding the way in, half the battle. When a kid's making herself a pain everywhere a pain possibly can be, if the home circumstances become clear, feel quite different. Same with Mummy. Once you see.

Way she stood over that cake, looking at it all ways, along and across, taking it all in, the shine of that icing—though it was too hard—the neatness of the writing. Hardshire

County Council and the date. That was really nice—though white on white? Little smile at the corners of her lips, very small but it was there, a softness round the eyes—and that was a good cake, certainly good—as a student's would've been extremely promising—though from what were supposed to be top-class caterers—but it brought out something in her.

Unexpected. Very.

Good food does that. We all need it. In a way, she needed that cake. Took time for picture to become clear. Thinking and thinking. It didn't go away. How she'd love a cake like that for herself. That she hidden it all these years. Childhood trauma? There was something. About Granma. She didn't like speaking about it—personal things too difficult, but they show, have to come out one or way or another. Home circumstances.

Aunt Peggy big part of the problem? Peggy meant well only Mummy couldn't see it. Drawn swords from the first. She was kind. Not loveable. Odd. Would seem obvious to love her? Maybe if things had been easier? Didn't understand her so couldn't love?

So Mummy? This cake now; taking it up to her. Good moist, sponge—fruit cake too rich for elderly stomach—iced with five-petalled violets. Understanding how they'll catch her eye. Seeing what's under the surface. Rationality. Reason. OK in their way. Love what really matters. Giving her what she'd love.

Jo coming too.

7

One hears a knock, calls, 'Come in' and they do, the pair of them. But no Bob with them. Why not? He said he was coming. Why don't they make themselves clear? Clarity is of the essence. She stares into a blank. One is perfectly capable of thinking. The difficulty is distance that can't be measured. Everything goes on the other side of a hedge.

One thing is clear—the second one's got her hands full of roses.

Father's clutching a clumsy bunch of flowers. It looks as if they will fall apart if he lets go. Mother's stands at the far end of the breakfast table, her face hardens, she says nothing. *Not in front of the child.* Later on the landing, strident to Ella. *Trying to get round me with roses for my birthday. Doesn't raise a little finger to help with his mother.* Betraying him to a servant.

That's clearly Joanne carrying these—whatever they are. Kate will have put her up to it. Sort of idea she would have. She's George's child though she came from one's own womb, wanting to be *normal.*

'Hallo Mummy, happy birthday.' How dark she looks sitting there in front of the window in that plain green frock, turning her head towards us, staring. You always imagine this time things will be different. And then those stark white walls are still glaring down, you still haven't made it, don't know what to say. 'We've arrived.'

Predictable answer. 'That's obvious, Kate, if I may say so.' But it's Jo the dark stare's focussed on. Her hands, clutching that bouquet.

'From the garden, Mummy, Canary Bird, d'you remember, from the arch next the pond?' Still that dull glare. 'We'll need a vase, Jo. There's probably one in the utility room—at the end of the corridor, turn right and it's on your left.'

Who's that at the door? 'Oh, do come in, Miss McDonald.' Now she's standing there, flicking glances and bobbing while she pours out words. 'So sorry, should have said when we were downstairs. We were so busy talking and it was Joanne who had them and I got involved with Mr. Lomas and the shop and the firing club. Should've known, of course, but as I didn't it was all so interesting it was only afterwards I thought.' She eases herself forwards in the direction of Jo. 'Those magnificent yellow roses. What a breath of summer.'

They are nice—but the excitement she manages—never cold is she? So nice someone who's never cold. Doesn't seem to realise buds won't have much scent, pushing her nose in among them like that.

'I do think roses are the most beautiful flowers.' So why's she blocking Mummy's view? *Through what wild centuries roves back the rose.* She really is the most extraordinary person—but not cold. 'And did you know the dog-rose was here in Roman times?'—though Mummy does look calmer—'They were used to them in their own country. Wore them at feasts.'—How on earth does she know all this?—'In the Bible too *the rose of Sharon'*—the way she pauses you'd think she was tasting the words—'such a wonderful name,' and then, after you can't imagine what to say back, she finds still more. 'You may think they're not the flowers a Scot should be backing but I can set aside national prejudice. There are other meanings too—fruit of the mystic rose—very strange—but'—at last she's managing to keep still—'you'll be wondering what I've come for. I thought you might be needing a vase.' She holds out a hand. 'Here let me take them. I'll arrange them for you.'

'Well—thank you, thank you so much—so kind—but Jo can do it.'

'Let Jo have all the time she can with her grandmother. It's no trouble at all.' Sharp eyes dart from the folds of a soft face. 'Well, I'll leave you now. You have everything else you need, haven't you?' She shuts the door so quietly and now it's just Mummy and Jo and you. 'Quite a character, isn't she?' Mummy staring at us across that table.

And Jo coming close. 'Want to put the cake down Mum?'

'Thanks.' What's that she's picking up from the table? Nice to get weight off arms. Place the box in the centre. Not the moment yet to unveil it. 'What's that you've got there, Jo?'

'Card, I'd guess. Looks like Bob's handwriting.'

'It's for your grandmother. Put it down.'

'Hasn't been opened.' One hip curved as she thrusts it out balancing on those heels. 'Shall I open it for you, Gran?'

She means well and the boots are better than those *platforms* she had to have last year. Clumsy and hideous. *You don't know anything, Mum. Big feet are sexy.* Sexy—oh dear. What a world they're growing up in.

'Look, isn't it lovely?' She looks so graceful now with her hair falling over her face, bending over Mummy showing her the picture, then looking inside. 'Best wishes from Bob and Janice.'

Creases sink into Mummy's forehead. Her voice is the height of crispness. 'Very kind of them.' Unfortunately Jo's not one to give up. 'It's really, really lovely. Look, Gran. They want you to keep in touch, you know, Gran. Bob came here a few weeks ago, didn't he?'

Where's she been to discover that? 'How d'you know?'

'Met him, didn't I, him and Jan, Saturday before last. They were going to *The Dog and Duck*.'

What a bland expression. You know it too well.

'Jan's lovely, isn't she, Gran? Really really lovely.'

Mummy's lips are working and Jo's staring. 'You do remember her—Janice, Bob's girlfriend?'

'They're always getting new girlfriends.'

'But they've been together ages, you know, Bob and Jan. Living together.'

'Jo—' Not safe to lay a hand on her arm.

'You must know. It's simply ages now.'

Whatever's got into Mummy, clenching her fists, pounding them on her skirt, speaking so fast. 'One's not interested in the arrangements of complete strangers. They're nothing to do with one.' Her face a mess.

'But Gran—Bob, you know Bob.'

'Never heard of him.' That's calmer.

'Yes, you have.' Jo's voice is twisting up in that superior way it does when she thinks you're stupid. 'My cousin. Bob.'

Get in quick—'Nasha's boy, Mummy.' What's that vague stare? 'You know Nasha?'

And now she flashes back, more like herself. 'Of course I know Natasha. Why are you being so stupid? One doesn't need to have Natasha explained. One knew her long before you were born.'

'Bob's her son.'

'Why didn't you say so? You should make yourself clear.'

'Yes, Mummy.'

Mum's sitting there in her square sensible shoes burbling on, trying to smooth things down. 'This really is a nice room.' Not what she said before but maybe she's taking a closer look. It's not bad, as rooms go. Curtains are wrong green. Shaz says their neighbours are putting in an avocado bath. I adore avocado. And those old armchairs look stuck to the ground. Bob and Jan's has those thin legs that lift it off the ground and make it look airy. This window seat's agony. Gran ought to get a bean-bag. Bob and Jan have one each. Get Mum to buy me one? Be really ace. Not bad the way the sun's sparkling along the shelves. Solid, those books. Gran's read them all. Takes some brains.

How could she not know Bob? How possibly couldn't she? She must do. Old. Old people forget. Their own family?

Bad day? Bit sleepy perhaps? Her face's sort of muzzy now, sort of gone soft. She's not coming back at Mum the way you'd expect. Gone inside.

The sun out there, the other side of the trees. Look at those branches, the way they're moving, like Nutmeg's shoulders cantering through the woods, his hooves thumping softly and the breeze like water on my arms. He's alone now in his field.

When I'm on him my feet hang close to the ground. Getting too big for him? Oh Nutmeg.

Trapped here, square box in a ghastly house, prison cell; but —grey shadows of leaves moving on the white wall, the wall almost yellow in one place and shadowed in another and the leaves reaching over the bed. Nice to sleep under leaf shadows? The outside getting in.

Gran looks more like herself, raising her eye-brows like that. Gives her an air. Quite something. Could I do it? Practise in front to a mirror? Use them on Mum? That'd be the day, she'd throw an absolute fit..

Mum's dress absolutely isn't right for her. Square neckline, big square collar, exactly the shape of those shoulders. Which are a complete, utterly total handicap. Only thing anyone can do is hide them. Plus the freckles on her neckbones. I was lucky to take after Peggy. *Long legs and decent shoulders.* Though my nose—

Suppose Mum couldn't get anything else. Bit of a problem. What d'you do when you're too old for fashion? You'd think there'd be shops for oldies. That pale blue's good though, with gingery hair. Not as strong red as Bob's.

Mum changed all the walls at Holmbush. Soon as we moved in. Said she couldn't stand the white. Looking at this room, I like it.

Gran has to remember Bob. How can't she?

8

'Bob is Natasha's boy?' Clarity is of the essence but leaves itch backwards and forwards. 'That red-headed creature?' Their heads turn. They gaze open-eyed

'Does one understand correctly—he's Natasha's son?' The leaves disrupt their faces.

'Yes.'

'At last. Thank you.' They make no attempt to get through the hedge, don't seem to notice it's there.

'And Janice is his girlfriend, Gran. They've been living together for ages but now they're going to get married. Isn't that great? Bob says he came here to tell you.'

One would remember something like that. Surely?

'Great?' Marrying? One works to understand people nowadays. 'And why do they want to do that?' Why's the girl screwing up her face?

'They love each other. Obviously. Otherwise they wouldn't have wanted to shack up together.'

Obviously—'Mind your manners.' She needs to be told to sit up too but clarity before all else. 'Make yourself clear.' This *shacking up*—Laura sitting on the floor hugging her knees. *The shackles of matrimony. The church was always the enemy of*

reason. 'The shackles of matrimony.' The other side of the hedge Kate stiffens. Her face goes hard. Neither of them has anything to say.

The girl pulls herself together first. 'Not shackles Gran. It's so obvious; anyone'd want to be free till they were absolutely certain. Only sensible thing. Then what they've chosen.'

Certainty, certainty—only in theorems. 'One's steady sitting on the floor.' Tracing triangles in the dust of the grate. The pair of them stare from a far off place where parallel lines don't meet and a problem keeps recurring. 'This Janice, who is she?'

This is weird, weird. She looks off into somewhere else and sort of murmurs these things as if they mean something. And the way she's clenching her fists. And I told her. Only three minutes ago. Plus she's met Jan. Years ago, Bob not there, Gran nosing across—my report or something—is she getting value for money from St. Margaret's? What Mum thought. Jan in bedroom next mine.

Jo can't really believe these half-baked ideas she's mouthing. 'Jan's Bob's girl-friend, Mummy.' And how does she know about Bob and Jan? Nasha said it wasn't official yet. Though it's about time. This about them going to see Mummy? Jo making it up?

Mummy looks brighter now, back to normal, what she said just now, how she can't remember Bob, a blip, slip of the tongue, one of those things we all do. Looking down now from that great height the way she always does. Fancy being glad to see it. Scent of lime flowers through the window.

Moment of quiet, thank Gawd and then suddenly Gran sits bang up straight. 'So you let them get away with it? Whatever would that woman say?' She's lost that flappy look.

Mum's not answering so I have to. 'What woman, Gran?'

'You know perfectly well. The one who goes round lecturing us about morals.'

'Lecturing?'

'She thinks she knows what's right—Mrs—'

'Mrs. Whitehouse?'

'That's what I said. Why do you keep repeating it?'

Mum's looking out of the window, pretending to be interested in the trees. Let who get away with what? Bob and Jan? Obvious to her how things were with Jan? I was a kid. Why doesn't she stand up for herself? For Gods-sake. I'm not afraid of the old crow. 'That's absolutely not fair, Gran.'

Thou hast conquered, O pale Galilean.' She murmurs in that far away voice but there's a sort of wickedness in it

'Gran?'

'That's what she said. *Thou hast conquered.*'

'Sorry Gran? Who?'

And Mum bounces it over her shoulder. 'Doesn't mean anything. Just poetry.'

Yeah, I can hear that and sometimes I quite like it. 'Is there more of it, Gran?' If she's in the mood. Any moment Mum's going to say drop it. But maybe a bit more would hang together. Have to find out, don't you?

Gran gives me a slow look, opens her mouth, waits, as if something's struggling in from a long way away and at last it arrives,

'Thou hast conquered, O pale Galilean,

The world has grown grey from thy breath.'

'Just poetry.' Mum throws the remark in again. 'Doesn't mean a thing.' But I look straight at Gran. 'Sounds lovely,' and she nods. 'What's it got to do with Jan?'

'Nothing,' Mum says, in a hurry again.

But Gran raises her head and murmurs, 'The hard-faced saints.' The vague look has come back.

I sit there, totally lost and she says it again, 'The hard-faced saints. No light behind the hard-faced saints,' in a strange voice that somehow reminds me of Kate Bush, coming from outside, from somewhere else, *Let me in, let me in.*

Mum's gone rigid and I can't think of any way of letting Gran in, whatever that means. Mum heaves a great sigh and turns. 'Don't take any notice, Jo. She hates Christianity, that's all, though she doesn't really mean it. It's just her way.'

Her way of what? She's looking at me again. 'Wisps of charity,' she says, 'your mother's got wisps of charity.'

And you're letting out wisps of sense, I think, but what she said sounded rude so I sit up and let her have it full in the eye. 'Stop criticising Mum.'

'Drop it, Jo, do.' Though she sounds pleased.

'Gran,' I say and lean forward and touch her knee. 'Gran, look at me,' and she does. There's something between us. 'Gran, what are you on about?'

'You can think,' she says suddenly. 'Your mother's hopeless but you've got a mind.'

May have or not. Not for me to judge and why does it matter? Wouldn't want to be an egg-head.

Then suddenly she's away again. 'Where's she hiding? Why didn't you bring her? No child? Never a child? Where's she hiding that child?' And Mum looks totally appalled as if she's woken up in loony-land. I flounder for a moment—well I'm totally, utterly gobsmacked—and then it comes back in a flood about Jan and that baby; years ago but it all came over me in a rush, how I let myself dream of a child that had been only just there—I was such a kid then—but listening to her it came back same way it came back last week when I wasn't listening to Miss Armstrong and all of them debating and Miss Armstrong told me to wake up and take part but all day, in the dull parts of lessons, I bathed and fed and played with that baby and tried out names. Which was silly. Three years later and it still came back, so I couldn't pay attention, knowing that kid had gone missing and now whatever children Bob and Jan might have in the future wouldn't be that one. That one had gone. Staring out the window—remembering that kid that was me looking at

Jan and thinking, one day I'll have one inside me. *Sorry Miss Jones. What did you say, Miss Jones?*

'Gran, Jan never had a child.'

'Why not?' This time she sounds completely on the ball.

She must know how it's done. Obviously not what she means. 'Not the right time.'

Suddenly she throws me completely. 'And you knew?'

I glance at Mum and see she's staring at me. 'Well—'

'And you Kate?'

Mum's goes blank, staring, straightening, shaking her shoulders. Then, almost pleading, 'It's not easy. You do what you can for the best.'

'Wisps of charity,' Gran says again and this time it sounds meant.

Mum turns and stares out of the window sitting with her legs apart and her toes turned out like a duck. Quack, quack.

Quack, quack the pair of them. *You do what you can for the best?* Something to help Jan? But—?

Odd that, in the toe of my boot, way that light bit stays in the same place. Can twist it round and round, point toe, heel down, now up. Still there. Mum exactly as always—mass of freckles across the backs of her hands.

What she said—about Jan—if she meant what it sounds—OK if someone else said it. someone younger, more up to date. Different kind of person. Absolutely, totally right then. Not Mum. She's always said the opposite. Laid it down. *Circumstances don't change what's right.* Should stick to it. Can't suddenly change your ideas, change sides.

Though great really, wanting to look after Jan—having her to stay, letting her go ahead, not letting on—but—not sort of thing—Mum's into. Can't help being old-fashioned—like her hair—way it's rolled tight in against her neck. No-one scrapes it in that way now. But she does. *Your Mum sounds so inhibited, Jo. Yours any better?*

Actually all over the place, oozy-woozy? Tackle Gran instead. 'They're getting married soon.'

Wisps of charity. She sets up perfection. All your best efforts only *wisps? We have erred and strayed* but there is no walled path, the straight and narrow—Janice and Bob—a mess at that time, students, nowhere to live. Jo coming up to an age? But not today, not just now. Sit up and take charge. 'I really don't see what Janice and Bob's affairs have to do with your Gran's birthday.' There's the cake, not perfect but OK, innocent, an innocent, shining thing, still hidden in its box when it's the whole point of everything. 'It's time we all had a cup of tea. I've brought a packet of your favourite Darjeeling, Mummy.'

'Marriage—'

'Your favourite Darjeeling. You know you love it.' She must be tired.

'One gives in when one ought not.'

'Come on, Jo. Help me get the cake out of its box.' Mummy was always out of the house, doing exactly what she liked.

'Gran, they're doing what they really want.'

Mummy's tired enough without Jo going on. Look at the pair of them straight-backed, obstinate, dark against the window, staring at each other. Why, why did you bring Jo? Today of all days when you'd do anything to keep Mummy happy. And Jo—all those years ago, she knew about Jan and kept it quiet? Never let on she'd met Bob and Jan in Gilbridge. How much else? 'The crockery's in that little cupboard next the bureau, isn't it, Mummy?'

Mummy outlined against a tangle of distant branches, her face grey. And just look at the way Jo's shoved her hands into her pockets. How many times? and stubbing her heels against the carpet.

'I'll just squeeze past to get those cups.' Good gracious, now they're in your hands, how many months since you unpacked them for her, arranged them neatly on these cramped shelves? 'Haven't had them out since you've been here, have you Mummy?' So dusty already. 'I'll take them down the utility room and give them a quick once-over. But before I do that, Jo do stop talking and give me a hand with the cake.' When she holds her head that way it's hideously Mummy.

9

Where's Mum got to? Way you can disappear in this place. Left's the way we came up—so right. 'Here I am.'

Severe look. 'You should've stayed to talk to your Gran.'

'She's in mummified mode.'

'Meaning?'

'Sits there staring at the air.'

'Nonsense.' She turns to the tap and tests the warmth of the water. 'But if you are here you might as well give me a hand.'

Not what I usually want to hear but just now—'Sure.'

She brightens at that. 'Well then, two pairs of hands—back in half the time.' Let's-make-the-best-of-it mode.

But I'm not aiming to get back too soon. 'Hey, I do like this on the table. Contac is it?' Smooth, thin, mustard circles on an avocado background. 'Jazzes the place up. Don't you think so, Mum?' Needs it too, all these glum cupboards, ancient gas-ring, which you don't need because there's a decent-looking jug-kettle. And she stops with cups piled in the basin, one hand on the tap, gazing into my face. 'What d'you mean, Jo?'

'Contac? You must know Contac, this sticky stuff, comes in rolls, for covering tops and things—'

'About Gran.'

'Sitting, gone off somewhere else, not really looking.'

She fiddles with the tap. 'She's tired.' Louder this time.

'Sort of flappy look, like a butterfly—not sure where it's going off to.'

'I've no idea what you mean.' Tight-stomach-mode. 'Could've found something to say, if you'd tried.'

She's turned on the tap so no need to answer in the noise. She's using too much washing-up liquid. *A little's enough. No need to drown the place in foam* and now look at her and beyond her outside the window the tree-tops are stirring. Nutmeg, alone in his field, Shaz at home, doing something with her Mum, me wasting the afternoon here. Mum plonking cups on the drying board. 'Come on, Jo—'

Pick up a cloth, wave it in the direction of the first cup.

Odd, isn't it, Mum's freckles, all the way up her arms, brown ants scurrying in and out of the foam as she dips her hands and raises them, her skin coarse. Mine's better, smoother, and shining across the wrist-bones. Her's brown and hairy like tree roots. Kind of strong though? Mine, in twenty years time? Gawd only knows. Mum's ideas now, rooted, rooted and fixed.

'Wakey-wakey.'

What? Oh. 'OK, Mum, OK.' Where's that blasted cup? Anything to keep her happy. 'Mum—' go on rubbing

—'when you and Dad got married, made a big difference, did it?' Sex and all that of course. *You should wait.* But those words they make you say, you have to stand up and say them so everyone can hear, some of the girls say too big—and clothes etc, everyone staring, first your back, then your front. 'Everyone says it's a wonderful day. How was it Mum? Was it great?'

You'd think that was a straightforward question but it's dither mode.

Couldn't help hearing, nothing else possible, she probably wanted to be heard—her saying something there was no need for her to say, not then, not there in the porch, us standing, new ring gleaming on fourth finger, John's arm thank heavens, and Mummy refusing Bill's hand, her voice ringing out, making sure everyone would hear, Robert and Agnes only a few yards away wondering what kind of family's this their son's marrying into? *Well, vicar, I trust the next time one finds oneself inside a church it will be for a funeral.*

Why did she have to say that? Bill wasn't used to her. Can't say in advance, my mother can be a bit outspoken? And when she comes out with something that seems to make no sense? Had heard it before, of course, over and over till she agreed to come, so knew. Better if she'd stayed at home? Don't even think that. Very good of her to come. Really. And he took it very well, nice man, looked at her very slowly, smiled, *I'm sorry, Mrs Lomas. I'm not quite with you.*

Since your theologians have decided, quite correctly, that God is dead, one is looking forward to attending his funeral. Bill burst out laughing, nice of him, thank goodness, thank goodness. All the same.

But after all it was all us, not her. 'Yes, Jo, it was wonderful.'

Don't-argue-with-me mode. No need for that. *'Wonderful?'* Doesn't need that tone. Not making herself clear. Trees swaying outside the window. Shaz not coming ever again. Mum in that dull blue suit, dull 'sensible' shoes pouring the water out of the bowl, wiping it dry. placing it upside down in the sink.. Oh Gawd. But suppose, just think, she and Dad—? Covering up? Can't believe a thing she says this afternoon.

'Hallo, Miss Ingram, you look lost.' Feet taptaptap, blackbird dashing across a lawn. 'Such a labyrinth this house, isn't it? I was never any good at mazes. Some sort of special skill, I think. Ancient people thought they could meet gods in mazes. Strange, isn't it? There, that's the door of your room, Miss Ingram.'

Caught Mum's eye. Even she can see what's funny in that. But who is that woman? The one Dad said, *Why do they have that woman here?* Who wants to go to Andover. Didn't get a word in this time. 'What she doing here Mum?'

'Who?'

'You heard. The one who's mad.'

'Don't talk like that.'

'Dad said *gaga*.'

The don't-argue-with-me look. 'Your Dad would never say that.'

'Heard him, didn't I?'

'He'd never have said that.'

'He did. Oh Gawd, Mum, you were there.'

'I really don't remember.' Deep sigh. Silence, then, 'Your Dad says she was a very able woman.'

'How come?'

'He acted for her. When he died her father left her the house and her brother tried to get the will over-turned. Your Dad used to come in saying how level-headed she was, no problems with the ins and outs of that will. Too complicated, he said, not phrased properly. He wouldn't ever have allowed old Mr. Ingram to draw it up the way he did.'

'So who did?'

'Your Dad never criticises his partners.'

'Oh sh—sugar, Mum.' Take her eye off from collecting up the cups. 'So what happened—to drive her mad?'

Deep sigh, picking up the tray. 'Mum—'

Pause, wait. She's put it down. 'Nothing happened, not that I've ever heard of.' Pause again, frowning—dodging? 'Told you before. Why d'you have to keep going on about it? It's just something—that happens to some people. They begin to forget.'

'Not just forgetting, she's barmy, Mum, totally barmy.

Frowning, lips tightening; got her.

'Jo—' a little desperate breathy voice—'it happens—sometimes—to some people. Their brain seems to break down. There's no 'Why?' It just happens. You have to accept it.'

'Oh, I see.' But I don't. Gran with eyes vacant as the wings of a cabbage white. 'Gran's too brainy, isn't she?'

Mum goes ballistic. 'Who said anything about Gran? This has nothing whatever to do with your Gran. She's exhausted, that's all. I can't imagine what Miss McDonald was thinking of, arranging all that fuss at lunchtime, wearing her out when she knew we were coming. It was obvious Gran would need all her energy for the afternoon.'

'Didn't sound anything much.'

Deep breath. 'Old people get tired very easily. You can see the state she's in. Surely to goodness you noticed, Jo? Completely worn out so she can't think straight, I'd no idea, really no idea at all, Miss McDonald could be so inconsiderate.' She turns a glare.full in my face. 'As for what you seemed to be saying, don't you go round suggesting that sort of thing. You should respect your Gran. Whatever would Miss McDonald think?'

'If she's so useless, why bother what she thinks?'

This is a rotten day. Mud on Nutmeg's pasterns. Been there a long time. The Downs never ever the same for the rest of time because of Shaz. Mum in patience mode, piling things onto the tray with her back to me. Deserves to be shocked. 'You and Dad, Mum, before you got married—like Bob and Jan? Bet you did.'

That makes her swing round. 'I'm sorry?'

'Trying things out, only way to be sure.'

This time it really is icicle mode. 'You know perfectly well that's quite unthinkable. Your Dad and I are Christians.'

'Only logical thing. You'd have to.'

'Logical? Logical? Where'd you get this idea things ought to be settled by logic? Logic doesn't decide what's right or wrong.'

Keep her hair on. Only said what I thought. And now she's leaning towards me, almost spitting. 'Don't you go picking up your Gran's clever-clever ideas. Don't you dare, I tell you.' Now bringing herself together, solid, sensible shoes almost denting the floor. 'She sounds as if she knows everything but she doesn't understand a thing.'

'Yes, Mum.' Or is it no? Gran's not stupid.

10

It's all too much for Jo. Shouldn't have made her come. Selfish. Wanted her company. But her Gran, she has to respect her Gran whatever. Who's sitting there in her chair, perfectly herself—all Jo said just nonsense—sitting up, watching you lay tea-pot, cups, plates on the table beside the box. Now, focus on the cake. Pull off cling-wrap, reach in, lift and the cake rises on its strip of cloth—wobbles—hold it steady, steady, lower it onto the plate, there. Tilt it a little with the left hand, with the right pull out the cloth from underneath. So, what d'you think? But you don't say it, only watch her staring eyes. An innocent, shining cake. Now for the candle holders, measure the space with your eyes, each one exactly half-way between two violets, one, two, three ...eight. That's it. Not bad at all. Slide in the candles, fat fingers you, these candles so small.

Gran's fixated, staring at Mum's fingers. 'The spider's web,' she announces.

What the heck? What the blooming heck? Completely off her rocker. 'What web, Gran? There's none here.' Mum looks totally, utterly gobsmacked.

'The spider's web,' Gran says again. There's something in her voice. Is there one we've missed—top corner? Back of the fire? She's fixated on white, would want the place spotless. 'Really can't see one.'

She notices me. 'The cobweb,' she says again and it sounds as if it's haunting her. 'What cobweb, Gran?' Mum clenching her hands.

'In the corner of the tall window,' she says kind of dreamily but at the same time as if she's seeing it. 'If one looks one sees all the sections are quadrilaterals.'

I'm totally, utterly lost.

She suddenly goes off into the I'm-the-one-who-knows-everything mode. 'You know, I suppose what a quadrilateral is?'

'Course.'

Her eyes slip away again. 'It looks circular but it's made of quadrilaterals.' What is? Oh the web, yeah—last September with rain-drops on it—and suddenly I get what she's on about, though not why. 'Yes. Gran, it is—' and her eyes swing back again a little brighter, though she still seems to be looking at something far away. 'The structure of the world,' she says and I'm thrown again but she seems to think she's really said something. 'Geometry built in,' she says staring into the air and I'm slowly catching up.

'The Downs,' I say, which is pretty daft but I've suddenly seen the point of trig with a kind of vision of the Downs seen from on top, a web of trig points, triangles running from one to another and then my mind suddenly jumps to a side view, skeletons stripped of their chalk, each one simply a post, Meldenham Beacon one height, Blackett Hill another, bit spooky—but true—not something made up in a book. It's absolute facts. Our eyes meet and we sit looking at one another, taking one another in.

Airy-fairy talk. As if any of it mattered. 6 oz flour, 3oz marge, all maths needed. Rub fat into flour = pastry.

'Come here, Jo, you can light them.' Mummy tightens, cold-faced. Could it all be an act? Underneath she must have always wanted a cake and fuss. We all do. Jo leans forward with the lighted match, hair falling over her face. 'Be careful with your hair—' and she sweeps it back behind her ear with the left hand, the right holding the flame steady sending points of light across the icing, Mummy watching. And now all the flames are dancing in their ring, steadying, eight of them, lifting themselves up toward the ceiling.

Mummy throws back her head. 'Won't let you. No—no—you shan't. Won't have my hair curled.' Gritting her teeth, frantic—but—?

Jo stands, open-eyed.

Own fingers pressed between each other, against each other. Shoulders, tummy rigid.

'Gran...Gran.' Jo speaks the way she does sometimes to Nutmeg when you've felt like saying, 'Stop crooning to that animal,' but now—voice trying to smooth over its hesitations—'Your hair's fine as it is—' wrinkle between her eyes.

'Don't want it curled.'

Stand. Look at her face. At last, words. 'Let's have a cuppa. Your favourite Darjeeling, Mummy.'

Jo still looking away but she reaches out a hand for the cup, brings it safely down to a place on the table beside her Gran. Thank God.

Grand girl who isn't afraid, who's standing now between one and the flaming horror—not simpering Sophie, not the church-warden's *nice little girl,* not Ella. One can uncurl. Where is this? One's been here before. That's one's bed. That's father's bureau. What day is it?

Things aren't as they should be. There seems to be something, more than a distance, a permeable blockage, one can only call it a hedge, that stands in the way, interferes and they're the far side of it, the pair of them, Kate and that girl who seems to think one would like some tea, girl, otherwise, with a head on her shoulders, who can think—wrong-headed of course—in the grips of the zeitgeist—but potentially teachable—one's grand—grand, they say—this one—grand girl who can think—one hasn't met many—And did one? Yes, it's certain—one succeeded extracted her from Kate's grip—ensured a good education Kate always snivelled—one tried to show her beauty, rationality, the calm behind appearances and she snivelled child of one's own womb and she snivels—distant now the far side of a ring of flames, unsteady fractals—trying to be Mother.

All to do now—pick up the knife, cut the first slice. Icing will give way gently. It's not hard. The inside moist, but firm. Hour and a half at Mark 4. The texture will be right.

Drive the knife in and Mummy's watching. This is the best cake you've ever made and it's all for her.

Oh Gawd, not getting any better. Wanna go home. At once. Now. Nutmeg with more sense than the pair of them put together. Alone in his field, mud on his fetlocks. And I'm stuck here. Oh Nutmeg, Nutmeg.

One speaks, the words go through the hedge and turn obliquely. A few minutes ago they flowed. One met the old arguments and was in command. These now are refracted off a world where Kate and Joanne stand, giving their minds to tea—*your favourite Darjeeling*—as if one cared, as if an iced cake could be important. Kate preening herself. One's own daughter turning her face away, pretending she sees nothing. But she does. She's slowly revolving her observations, trying to fit them into her *normal* world. One came to this house hoping not to have to see her doing that, but she's followed. Imagines a cake is central. All one's life one's tried to make her understand. Small children; so difficult. One hoped, hoped indeed, tried, but no. In the end one has to admit failure, as honesty requires. Mrs Forster knew how.

And now she's not blown out the candles. She's not on top of things trying to cut the cake without blowing out the candles, removing just one so she can cut that significant slice. What a big thing she makes of it.

That tea's uncomfortably close to one's elbow but when one pushes it's clear the girl has put the cup too close to the edge.

'Quick, Jo, rescue the cup. There it is, behind the chair. Be a dear, will you, go and fetch a cloth from the utility room?'

'Yes, Mum.' And out. Whoops. Oh, the quiet of this corridor. Seemed spooky, but now.

Not totally quiet. Little gasps. Somewhere, someone's crying. Half-open door on right. Slide past into the utility room which is more like home, hanging cupboards, electric kettle, Fairy liquid, bright curtains, plastic but even so. Garden down there's a bit of mouldy grass and a few boring trees. Out of doors all the same. Sun. Wind. Couple of old bats down there sitting on deck chairs, rabbiting on, and now flinging their heads back, laughing. Couple of old bats, laughing in this place? Whatever can they find here to laugh about? Lucky them. Look as if they're friends.

When Nutmeg hears me coming he whickers, comes trotting up to the gate, puts his head over. He called this morning, to the other ponies, both lots of them, in Daphne Manners' field and the ones we met in the wood. They called back. Liking their own kind. You need your friends.

Him on his own. All week. Maybe a couple of parties come past. He'll call, they'll answer. Maybe he'll come to the gate and watch, see them disappear. Oh Nutmeg—perhaps—

Daphne Manners wants him. She's said so. To be ridden by any old person.

Jade, Carly, Shaz, Debs, Kev—that great wally. All of them having a go? Most anyway, summer evenings after school. Not Kev mostly? Afraid girls would do something better than him? All of us friends then.

Not the same as a riding school. Not so different. Had to show them, didn't I? Not that they took much notice. Jade and Carly hanging onto his mane, having a great time screaming, so Kev would look.

Shaz a natural. Gentle, loving him as much as I do.

Let him go? Not mine any more? Can't imagine—the emptiness. Couldn't. No way I could live without him. Him without me? Looking over the fence of that field wondering why I wasn't coming? Trotting to the other ponies for comfort? His own kind?

I'd miss him, desperately, desperately. But he'd always know me, wouldn't he? Come to me more than any of the others. Mrs Manners wouldn't let them hurt him. Heard her, old bag, doesn't half yell if they tug on the mouth.

If I stood on the other side of the fence at the bottom of her field he'd come to me.

Or—what if—Saturdays only free day—what if I got a Saturday job—mucking out but still—Shaz not the only one—she'd see—tell her, wouldn't I? Get to ride him? Bet I could handle that rangy grey too. Show Shaz she's not the only one with money of her own.

Nutmeg, you wouldn't be more friends with the other ponies than you are with me?

Your own kind. Like Shaz and me. On the lawn down there two old ladies still rabbiting on. Ooze off down to Shaz's place? Tomorrow? Risk her auntie being there?

Find a cloth now before Mum goes ballistic.

Whoever it is inside that room, still crying. Their own business. But all this time? Something really, really bad? Their own business, I said. Leave them to it. Tell Miss McDonald? What use'd she be? This place so quiet, except for that ghastly grunting.

Put his head toward the jump, firm in my knees. He won't run out. Come on, Jo, take a breath, only one finger and the door moves. It's that old lady, the one who's dying to go to Andover. In the chair by the window, face in her hands, looking up now through trembling fingers, eyes wet, pale, the skin round them white and shiny. An old person crying. Ghastly, ghastly, millions of times worse than a baby. Back out—sorry, this is the wrong room. But—but—firm in knees. 'What's the matter? Can I help?'

She's taking away the fingers, letting them trail across her lap, turning up towards me flabby pink cheeks, a long mouth. 'They won't let me go to the party.'

Who? Miss McDonald? What in the whole bloomin' world she talking about? No party here except for Gran and that's not much of a party. She's barmy, away with the fairies Dad says. No hope of getting sense out of her. Leave her. But she's looking up, pale blue eyes. Faded? Her face—and her body, crumpled like a worn-out vest—her whole face, turned up, eyes steady now, glued on me. 'We're having a party, just a very small one, would you like to come?' Can't leave her, whatever.

A small, wobbly smile.

Let myself in for it, haven't I? 'Come on. I'll help you up.' No weight. Incredible. At least she's steady on her pins. 'There you are, that's it.'

11

What on earth's that girl up to? Mummy on your hands—after she's—it almost looked as if—not an accident. Something in the way her hand moved. Mummy would never push a cup off the table, deliberately, on purpose; impossible but—and the sun touching roofs and tops of walls the other side of the road, glass flashing through the trees. The opposite side lit up, when this side's lost the light. Bookshelves pressing in. Mummy, hands clasped in her lap, straight-backed. The candles flickering, scent of lime-flowers.

Kate's so prim, knees pressed together, staring at that cake. Burn, burn. The light of the flames. One needs to look away but it's the shortest distance between two points. The eyes locked onto a straight line. Wisps of smoke rise from candles. The hard-faced saints. One sees them through of flickering candles. Staring down.

The reason should be in command but the eyes fix themselves on what one doesn't want to see.

Facts have to be faced. Kate's stupid. Stupid. *Happy birthday?* One's done one's best to make things clear. *Many happy returns?* One hopes very much not. How can one's own daughter be so incredibly stupid?

What's that in the corridor? Jo's voice—and? And?

A hand swinging the door open. Dark blue cardigan. Dark blue skirt. Scraps of hair. Bent figure, shuffling. Jo's head over her shoulder. Bringing her in here? That mad woman? Bringing her in here? Why? Why?

'Brought someone, Mum.' Girl sounds cheerful while the mad woman, raises her head, treats us all to her eyes, stares at the lit-up horror, shuffles, towards the gap in the hedge where one can't run away from the nightmare. Totally clear. Reaching out an asbestos hand, almost touching the flames. 'Pretty. Pretty.'

Kate pulls her arm. 'Take care, Miss Ingram.'

Who? Is that true? Truths have to be faced. She was Miss Ingram once. And one was Alice, then Lomas. One sank into the fifth dimension, recognised fractals in the garden, interpreted the County Council's accounts. Yes, surely one is Alice Lomas, behind this hedge where the wrong things make sense, where one watches someone who used to be Miss Ingram reach out like a small child to candles? She knocked and waited, only came in when called. Droopy brown tweed skirt, hands clasped *like to learn to drive mobile canteen.* Small for the job but she looked at one, eyes met. *I'll put forward your name.* A long time ago. How long? How long is time? It bends round on itself. In this room today she has to be prevented from putting her hand into flames. Gaga. Face facts. Don't run away from the words. *Off with the fairies.* How does it happen? She was a sensible woman. If she'd been stupid. A brain becomes soft. Off with the fairies the other side of a hedge? What one says makes them look blank. They turn, stare, look away. The hedge sprang in between. A creature roamed up and down behind it.

A little time ago talking to that girl it wasn't there. It was all clarity and reason. The search for them over a lifetime fortifies the brain. It is impossible for such a brain to fail.

*

What? Who? 'Jo—?'

She ushers old Miss Ingram in, one hand almost touching her shoulder. John says she was a fine woman but look now, reaching out like a child. Horrific—and yet somehow sweet, the candles lighting her face, her cheeks rising out of shadow, eyes a small child's, loving the cake. 'Take care. Don't burn your fingers.' Aunt Peggy's nails were scarlet, long and scarlet, beautifully shaped. These are plain and the fingers tremble, covered in bluish-white skin. 'Fetch a chair, Jo. There's one tucked away in that corner.'

Old Miss Ingram loves the cake so much. Must bring back memories. 'Would you like a piece?' Look, look, she's fascinated, watches every least fraction of an inch as the knife sinks in. A warmth spreads. Ease out the first slice, 'Look, Miss Ingram, d'you see? Should taste lovely.' Nice moist sponge, two layers of butter icing.

You really shouldn't have, Peggy. Mummy spoke levelly gazing down the length of the table. Now, today this 'Get rid of her.' The voice shrill, rising out of another universe. 'At once, I tell you.'

Jo looks devastated. Serve her right.

All such a mess. Come on, grit teeth, nothing more really than taking charge at a children's party. But that's what it isn't. 'She's not doing any harm, Mummy. Where's that cloth, Jo? Wipe the table can't you?' and your daughter takes that shocked face closer to her Gran, bending forward, softly rubbing polished wood, making a good job of it. 'Thanks Jo.' Give her a smile. Watch her face ease. 'There, that's nice, isn't it, Mummy?'

It's her eyes, fixed on you, not cold, almost entreating. 'She doesn't belong here. I won't have her.' What they say in the playground. You can't play with us.

But this is Mummy, raising her voice. 'Won't have her. Tell her to go.' She never raises her voice.

You've offered Miss Ingram a slice of cake. Look how her eyes are fixed on it. She must have it. and Mummy's hands rising in a way you've never seen, her eyes turning to you. Almost as if she's going to say, *It's not fair.* Don't let her. Mustn't let her. Have sorted these things out, many times. But this? 'Wait. She'll go as soon as she's finished.' Your voice soothing, trying to calm her the way you used to calm Jo when she hurled herself into your arms. How come? Habit takes over? And you? Me? Standing, taller, looking down and she's looking up as if I'm the only one who can help. 'It's OK, Jo. Your Gran's a bit tired.' That cynical look. Did you expect her to believe it? Oh well. 'Miss Ingram's going to drop her plate. Take charge, will you?'

But Mummy. Me and Mummy. A see-saw with me at the top end, my feet ready to push against the ground. I could bring it down, wham, fly up again and shake her off, leave her lying in puddles and mud. Trample on her. Small, stupid Kate. Who couldn't understand a thing but now understands everything, whose heart has suddenly leapt up to run her through with a hot, harsh upward jab, who, suddenly, could take off and fly. 'Miss Ingram's here, Mummy. We've offered her cake. She must have time to eat it.' And if Mummy doesn't like it—'Cut yourself a slice, Jo.'

'Kate, Kate, get rid of her, Kate.' She'll be crying soon.

What's eating Gran? *Rationality is of the essence* but what's this? Gran really, really clever, arguing with me, a little while ago, now this. Like that wail from another world, *Let me in, let me in.* Mum not raising a finger.

Shouldn't have brought the old bat? Seemed right. She was so utterly miserable. Just wanted to be kind. Nothing wrong with being kind.

Mum's not being kind. Not raising a finger. Leaving Gran out in the cold. Looking at her way Old Barnaby did at Emma when she slapped her down. She's got it in for Emma.

Mum's got it in for Gran? Not like that, doesn't have it in for people; bit soft normally, fussy—of course—well-meaning on the whole. Sharp-eyed now, watching the old lady crumble cake between her fingers, stuff a ball of crumbs into her mouth, gobble it down, the skin on her throat wobble as it goes down; tossing a remark over her shoulder, 'Cut yourself a slice, Jo,' and without bothering to ask, 'Gran probably won't feel like it.'

How's sweet icing going to sort out all this? 'Don't want any.'

'Get rid of her, Kate. Now, please, Kate.'

Mum still standing, straighter than usual as if she's shoving her feet into the earth. 'Just wait, Mummy.' Teacher mode. 'Lovely, isn't it, Miss Ingram? Take your time. There's no hurry.' Gently to a little kid. The old bat dropping crumbs all over her lap, letting them get down onto the carpet, Mum not turning a hair, watching her chew, beaming all over her face. Gran twisting her hands, panting.

At last—'Jo, wrap a bit more of the cake in cling-wrap for Miss Ingram.'

Thank Gawd. Thank Gawd. Something to do.

'Here's a little bit more to take with you, Miss Ingram. Jo'll see you back to your room.'

Mum seems to know how to get her off the chair, the corridor's so peaceful compared with that room, the footsteps are Miss McDonald's. Thank Gawd again, thank Gawd.

Must, must get round to Shaz's. Place. ASAP. For now slide off down to the utility room, open the window, look out. Oh Nutmeg.

A good cake, revealed when you cut it, nice moist sponge, two layers of butter icing, iced top and sides—not quite orthodox but how Miss Ingram loved it, crumbling her piece, making the crumbs into a ball, cramming the ball into her mouth, letting it rest there and dissolve, extracting every last bit of sweetness, her eyes fixed on the candles—you'd think she'd never seen anything like them before, that first magic birthday or Christmas and the child reaching out. When it comes to cake we're all children. *Take your time,*

Miss Ingram, take all the time you want, wanting to pat her shoulder. Forgot, just for the moment, seeing her so happy, *she was a very competent woman.* We're all children when it comes to cake. *Take another slice with you, Miss Ingram.* Taking no notice of Mummy, her face gone grey, staring at the candles, mouth gone slack, flopped open, watery eyes.

She turns them up at you. Appalling, most appalling moment ever. Floor shakes underfoot, air draws away. Stand in a vacuum beside the cake, looking down. If only could have done roses. Those flowers aren't warm, the colour of bruises, of many bruises and the white seems to be faintly stained, violet on the dark edge of the rainbow where it fades into rain, oozy-woozy, uncertain colour. No, thank you, Aunt Peggy? If only. The red hair-ribbon still in its box, tucked away, back of top right-hand drawer. Suitable for wild Irish Caitlin. Her blood surging now through you as you stand, looking down, someone who's stopped being Mummy looking up with watery eyes.

Blow out the candles, take this new voice you've just found, address it to Mummy. 'There you are. All gone.' Put the cake back on its strip of cloth. Lower it into the box. She watches every move and you love it. 'There you are, Mummy. All packed away.'

Could take it out again. And watch her. Gone now, your teddy bear. Boo. Boo, back now, the child laughing and laughing with her. But this is cold. *I can get you.*

The cruelty of children. You break them up. *Stop that. You should be ashamed.* Is it possible, are you capable of—? That long looking—they call it gloating—her looking up, horribly pleading and you, grown woman who calls herself Christian, commanded to love and making a stab at it, as much as is reasonable, as anyone could, not a saint, never pretended to be a saint—but what is this, this hot triumphant soaring? That doesn't care about love or forgiveness, which it ought to, which are what matter most but just now don't at all so long as it can have what it wants, that flame rising hungry inside you. Could you—you, mild, feeble little Kate, standing there in you dull, sensible shoes —*On my feet all day, They're killing me. Why don't I wear sensible shoes like yours?*—don't say, just think, looking at her—*because you're not dull,*—could you—?

Of course not, don't be silly.

'Jo will be back soon.' Sit down, wait. What's keeping her?

Heard other women—but they were letting themselves down. Thought so then, sitting in their sitting rooms, looking at their furniture, listening, trying to understand, sorry things had gone so terribly wrong for them. And they had. But so little to say; searching and searching. Not good with words. Their troubles so difficult. Yours—did you have any?—handle things with a little care. Luck too. Holmbush and Fairhurst. Daddy. *The Institute is really lovely, Daddy.*

Wild Irish Caitlin looking down on Mummy? Don't be stupid.

See the way she's curled back in that chair? Never seen her like that before. When she's on her own perhaps? Be alone a lot in this place. Holmbush too, perhaps? She sees me looking and straightens her back. How white the skin is round her eyes. An old woman's skin, almost transparent, shiny. Any old woman. She looks weepy.

Impossible. Not in her. Hasn't got what it takes. No. No. Can't say that. Don't say it. Just because you've never seen her. She won't cry. What would you do if she did? Suddenly becoming a baby. The world tilted on the wrong axis.

Mummy, terrified apparently—of candles on a birthday cake? This is all the most terrible mess. You're pincered, Mummy, Jo, are looking to you as if you're on top now and you can sort it out and the shadow of the leaves outside trembling across the wall. Has a wind got up? It's like pushing your way up through a thorn hedge, shoot seeking the light, pushing through though it's not completely what you want, the top generation now, shading the lower growth, exposed to wear and time.

Not alone. There's still John.

And Jo, if she'd only get herself back. Poor Jo. That warm heart of hers, landed her in the soup once or twice before. Must have got Miss Ingram back into her room by now. Whatever's the girl up to?

Stand up. 'I'll get this lot washed up Mummy.' She just stares. Collect them any way, cart them down the corridor. Apply a firm foot to the door.

So there's Jo's, her back at any rate. She's staring out of the window and as she turns—could she have been crying? No use going into things now. A bad, bad day.

Warm water runs into the bowl. Soothing.

'Gran on her own?'

'Why not? The cloths are behind you.'

'This is the cake plate, Mum. What you done with the cake?'

'Back in its box.'

She stops wiping, lowers her arms. 'So what we going to do with it?'

'Get on with the job. Take it home. What else?'

'You want to eat it?'

'Your father would like some.'

She wipes half-heartedly.

'Come on, Jo. We haven't got all day.'

'He can't eat it all.'

'For goodness sake—' Why can't she leave the subject alone? The whole of that topic—too late now, why bother? But look at that crumpled face. 'How about leaving most of it for the home? We'll give it to Miss McDonald. How's that?'

Brighter now. Thank heavens.

The hedge doesn't protect. Eyes reach through and one's shaking. Rationality's of the essence. Candles on a cake are more powerful. Kate should have known. One's made it clear and clear and clear. The room's full of anger, growling all round. Kate can't be so stupid. Can she?

Nobody could. She planned it.

She's evasive, no straightforward honesty in her—facts have to be faced, however painful. She's always gone behind one's back, always imagined one didn't know what she was up to though of course one did. She and her father plotting, the pair of them together. In that kitchen—she'll have swept one out of it though she doesn't tell—*Nothing's really changed, Mummy*—standing there stirring that cake, putting all her wiles into violet icing. She knew perfectly well. What she was doing.

One fell into her trap. She made things sway this way and that. Why do they swing? Why don't they stay? And Miss Ingram? Away with the fairies? Where do one's thoughts go? Reason nowadays not to be trusted? That cannot be possible. .

There she is now back again, pushing the door open with the front edge of the tray. 'So Kate, come to gloat, have you?' She stands there, mouth half open, silent. She knows. 'Nice little party you planned.'

Now it's that girl, running, kneeling in front of one, hands warm on yours. 'It's not Mum's fault, Gran, it was me, I brought the old lady.' Cheekbones the same shape as Kate's, the same eyes—but looking up, meeting one's gaze. 'I didn't mean to upset you, really, genuinely didn't. Just wanted to be kind. She was so unhappy.'

Kate the other side of the table. 'Unhappy? What d'you mean, Jo?'

'She was crying. Wanted to come to the party so I brought her. Nothing wrong with being kind, is there?'

This girl, though she's got Kate's eyes, can hear what one says. Gather up resources. 'One should trust in reason.' She looks hard, says nothing, Kate standing behind her, about to start bleating.

'I'll just put the crockery away, Mummy.' Good china that. 'From Wilson's. Kate, before the war.' She glares but handles it carefully. Quick but capable. Standing back again, holding herself better than usual. The other side of that hedge.

She announces, 'Time we should be going. I think we've left everything tidy.'

This time one can find that slippery formula. 'Thank you for coming.'

A long, wondering look. Honest—perhaps?

'I'll come again next week.' So that's clear. 'I'll ring beforehand so Miss McDonald can let you know.'

'I shall be delighted.'

Sitting up better by the end. Talking weirdly, so formal. But no ice. Not in her eyes, not in her voice. Who is this, who's looked up with runny eyes? Mummy without her ice?

And here's Miss McDonald at the foot of the stairs. The day's been too much. 'Perhaps—' shove a cake with flowers the colour of bruises at her with wooden arms and she tilts her head, takes it into her hands—'the other residents?'

'What a lovely idea, Mrs. Barnes. So generous.' She pauses. 'We'll cut it in slices and put them in with the other cakes for tea-time. There's no need to worry. Mrs.Lomas won't remember.'

Slices, passed round on a plate, *Happy Birthday* cut apart like *Hardshire County Council.* Why not? A splendid cake you'd thought—with white icing reflecting rain-cloud. But you thought then, *splendid,* though you shouldn't and now no-one to see. So many hours, so much thought. Hours standing in the kitchen getting it right, feet in *sensible shoes* killing you. The day fallen to pieces, everything crumbling lips threatening to crumble, these tiles underfoot letting you know life's hard. Love crumbling too. Hate even perhaps. 'Perhaps the staff could like some as well?'

'I'm sure they would.' Miss McDonald smiles gently through the gloom of the hall. 'So kind of you.' Words echo off dark panelling. 'Thank you so much.'

Cold air round your head and you have to say it, even if Jo's listening. 'There's one thing, Miss McDonald—' And she leans her head to one side, waits without bobbing. 'Some of the things she says—'

A gently enquiring tone. 'Not quite on the ball?'

'Odd. Too much on her own perhaps—? Or today—overtired. There was all that business at lunch-time.'

'More than that, isn't it?' That gentle tone again.

'Totally off course. Be real Mum.'

The height of this hall. The dark roof.

'Can't you make things easier for her so that—?'

'I'm sorry, Mrs Barnes.' She clasps her hands but her feet are firm against the tiles. 'Really sorry.'

Is she refusing? How dare she refuse? 'Surely Miss McDonald—'

But she looks you straight in the face. 'It's her mind, not quite right, not working the way it should. She's not tired but her thoughts are slipping, which must be terrible, can you imagine it? Especially for someone like her.' She firms up all over. 'But she's not mad, you know. It's a disease that affects the brain.'

'Disease?'

'It was first discovered almost a hundred years ago but somehow the news hasn't got out till quite recently.'

'A disease?' It helps to repeat the word. There's firmness there. 'Like measles?'

'Measles can cause blindness. It penetrates the brain and reaches the sight.'

'But this is thoughts.' Which run freely, inside or outside the head.

'It affects the pathways through the brain.'

Thoughts aren't things. They're spiritual. They run free. 'A disease?'

'I'm sorry, Mrs Barnes, a terrible disease. If only I could say something hopeful, but I can't, I really can't. There's nothing, nothing at all.'

Jo challenges her. 'If it's an illness there has to be a cure. Has to be.' And Miss McDonald smiles at her. 'I'm sure they're working on it, Jo. That's in the hands of your generation.' And Jo opens her eyes very wide and says nothing.

The brain's flesh. But thoughts? In what she says where are thoughts? Where is the soul?

'Mrs. Lomas, Mrs. Barnes, such a distinguished woman. She must have been brilliant.'

'Yes, I suppose so. Yes.' What happens to the soul? 'Her maths? Surely she can't lose that?' Is her soul in her maths?

'It always comes harder when someone's been so brilliant.'

What would she be without maths? Alive, so the soul not gone? If her soul's in her maths? Don't be stupid. Is your soul in your kitchen? In a way—no, somewhere else. Not part of the body. And thoughts, not part of the body though Miss McDonald talks as if they are.

But something is wrong. Mummy not quite herself.

'To lose anyone to that, to see them slipping away. You'll need courage—and so will she.'

'Lose? Is she going to die?'

She clasps her hands, stands firm, soft-voiced. 'Not die. Not now. Just slip away from herself. I'm sorry, Mrs Barnes, truly sorry—but you must suspect some of this already.'

'There is something wrong.' You've known and not known, spelled it out now plain and undeniable. But where is the soul?

'I've been reading an article in a professional magazine. The changes in the brain are irreversible.' Eyes which have sometimes frightened you by their sharpness are soft.

'Would it help you to see it? If you let me know next time you're coming I'll put it out for you.'

'It would be good—to understand.' But it won't tell you about the soul. 'Yes, to understand, thank you.' Even stupid Kate would like to get her head round something. For Mummy's sake.

You think that, believe it or not.

So you don't hate her? Not that sort of monster? 'And meanwhile?'

'She's proud, isn't she? Such a proud person.'

Distant. On a pinnacle.

'She won't thank us for making things too plain.'

'She's always preferred to face facts.'

A smile, the head tilted once more. 'I think she does, Mrs Barnes. But we'll come at it slowly. It's hard, very hard, not what everyone would expect, not what anyone would wish to hear—and old people, you know, it's strange but we often find it so—aren't always most open with their children.'

Who will she be, off that pinnacle?

'We'll take care of her here and help her towards—whatever understanding's possible.'

'And then?'

'We'll have to see. Just have to wait and see. Tell me, Mrs Barnes, what did she say when you left her?'

'She'd be delighted to see us.'

'Then believe her. She's very truthful.'

'Yes. Yes, she is.'

Out of this door and into the car and as you let in the clutch: 'Many, many thanks, Jo. I couldn't have managed without you.' Take it the mutter means she's pleased.

For Mummy's sake. You thought that. Didn't think you could come up to it. So you must be able. Some trace of real love? They say children always love their parents whatever. *Keep families together.* And, always in the background, there'll be John. One hundred per cent. Whatever.

At last, the lane leading to Holmbush where Jo gives the day another twist. 'By the way, Mum, I'm getting a Saturday job.'